M000079825

First Paperback Edition. Press.

Website: www.samcalvo.com

Instagram: @samcalvoauthor

Email: sam@samcalvo.com

ISBN (paperback): 978-1-7358735-4-1
ISBN (ebook): 978-1-7358735-5-8

". . . an expertly crafted series of short science fiction stories bound together by deeply relatable themes. Each story offers a unique perspective into the human condition as well as compelling insights into where humanity could be heading."

—**Amadeus**, Beta Reader

". . . a haunting exploration of the human mind and what it means to truly be 'free.' With interweaving stories that combine elements of horror, dystopian and psychological fiction, the book plants itself firmly in the realm of the uncanny."

—**Meg McIntyre**, Founder of McIntyre Editorial Services

www.mcintyreeditorial.com

"Never once did I accurately predict the end of any story. There hasn't been a novel that has reached the deep corners of my mind like this one"

—**Brenna Fowler**, Beta Reader

"The characters in Addison's Wake leave an indelible impression. Though disturbed, beleaguered, and caught in the dark, they each remain stubbornly curious and hopeful. Across multiple genres and environments, their *haunted and harried voices warn of the frenzied dysfunction of our modern world, while clinging to aspirations that may still be dashed to pieces."*

—**Joseph Goddall**, Author of What the Bird Sees in Flight

www.jrgoodall.com

"I loved this book, so many twists and turns that I was never expecting. A gripping read."

—**Hannah Emcez**, Beta Reader

"Sententious and engaging . . . a streak of morbidly dry humor runs through most of the stories. Some are quasi-serious; some are simply funny."

—**Danny DeCillis**, Founder of the online publication, Check Please!

The Found

"I don't like it," Ellie declared.

Mordecai was taken aback. "What do you mean?"

"I don't like it."

"What do you *mean* you don't like it?"

Ellie looked up at the blazing halo and covered her eyes with her arm. "The light is very bright. It hurts my eyes."

After walking over the stone bridge, Mordecai and his little sister Ellie stood at the edge of the only known lookout point outside of Macrosanti. In front of them was a landscape in a part of the world that had no name—a barren wasteland for many miles until, if you squinted hard enough, a forest of trees and a range of snow-flecked mountains nestled into the edge of the horizon. Puffy clouds patterned an azure sky and a halo of blinding light radiated from above.

"It hurts mine, too," Mordecai said to her. "I don't think our eyes are used to it. Just don't look at it."

"What's the point of it if we can't look at it?"

"I don't know. But this is what everything else is. This is the world."

Ellie placed her delicately manicured hands on the stone ledge and gazed at the landscape.

"So *this* is The Found?"

"Yeah, it is."

"Why do they call it that?"

"The patrollers call it that."

"But nobody ever finds it?"

"It's ironic."

"Oh."

A rude wind breezed past them, and tiny goosebumps formed on Ellie's arms. A shiver went down her back.

"It's so cold. My teeth are chattering. Do you think they'll turn up the heat?"

"No, they can't do that."

"Why not?"

"The climate-control web isn't part of this. It's only inside Macrosanti."

Ellie glanced back at the enormous geodesic dome from which they came. Their friends and family were back there. The stone bridge went right back into Macrosanti through a little opening. It wasn't so cold back there. Ellie let out a few little coughs.

"The air is so thick. I feel like I'm breathing smoke."

"We're just not adjusted to breathing this air," Mordecai assured her. "It's natural."

"It hurts."

"It's *natural*."

"But I like the air back home."

Ellie pointed back to Macrosanti and Mordecai became agitated.

"It's not home, Ellie!" he snapped. "It'll never be our home. The people there are not living. They are dying."

"But it's nice there. Mommy and Daddy are there. All of our friends are there."

"It's not real, Ellie! It's not how the world should be."

A ragged ladder dangled over the side of the stone lookout all the way down to the wasteland floor. Ellie peered over the side and curled herself into a fetal position on the ground.

"I don't *wanna* go!" she cried. "I don't wanna go down there! I don't wanna leave!"

Mordecai couldn't blame her. The lookout was the harshest place they'd ever seen. He tugged at her arm.

"C'mon, Ellie. You have to get up."

"I don't wanna go!" she cried again.

"I know it looks like nothing, but past the mountains there's a forest, and we can go—"

"I don't wanna *go!*" she screamed.

Mordecai looked back at the two men at the other end of the bridge. They were wearing silk clothes with the emblem of Macrosanti plastered across the chest—the uniform of the patrollers. They were too far away to read their facial expression, but Mordecai knew they were snickering at them. *Nobody goes down the ladder*, he imagined them joking to each other. *And even if they did, they wouldn't survive. They're just kids.*

Ellie wouldn't budge, and Mordecai knew he couldn't force her to leave Macrosanti and live with a brooding resentment that would hang over her head like a perpetual storm cloud. He put a supportive hand on her bare neck, which was soft to the touch. They shared the supple skin of Macrosanti.

"The world behind you isn't your world," Mordecai softly said to his crying sister. He pulled a small tattered book from his jacket pocket and opened it up. "Look, see this here?"

"You already showed me your stupid book!" Ellie hollered. "I'm sick of hearing about it. It's all you talk about and it's not true. Mommy said so already."

"She's never been here. Never seen this," Mordecai said. He flipped through the book until he reached a page and revealed it to Ellie.

"Look."

"I don't wanna look."

"Just look, Ellie!"

The page looked like a map, except that Macrosanti was shown as a tiny dot in the middle while the rest of the page was covered in foreign clumps of brown and green with unreadable markers. Ellie had never seen a map that showed Macrosanti so small. In fact, she had only seen maps of Macrosanti itself.

"Do you see all this?" Mordecai said, pointing to the brown and green clumps. "This is the rest of it. The book says that the natural world is—"

"I don't care about your stupid book!" Ellie hollered. "That's all you ever talk about anymore, that stupid book. I miss Mommy and Daddy. I want to go home. I don't care about your stupid book, I don't care about the map, just burn the horrible thing!"

Mordecai sighed. "Ellie, you need to understand—"

"I don't want to understand anything! That book has loosened your tongue and it's made you say such awful things. I hate this place, I wanna go home!"

Mordecai accepted and stuffed the book back in his jacket. Ellie didn't talk like the other kids. Mainly because Mordecai didn't talk like the other kids, and she was always with him, so sometimes she talked like him. Soon she would start to talk like the others—so would Mordecai—but Mordecai knew somewhere deep inside of her was a rebellious spirit, and once she found it, they could finally go home.

"Okay, Ellie," he said softly. "Let's go back."

Mordecai took Ellie's elegant hand in his, connecting their delicate, silky skin as they walked back on the stone bridge toward Macrosanti where every day was the same. The light-sphere inside shone bright. The food was always pleasant on the tongue, and everyone inside was alive. Everything was alive and nothing died.

Nothing was allowed to die inside of Macrosanti.

The dome was impenetrable.

There were no cracks so that not even the faintest of suffering could seep through. Deprived of a true mind and body and soul that's molded through hardships. Excesses of everything that stimulated the senses all the time, enclosed in an artificial habitat surrounded in granite and chrome towers with sterile streetscapes, everything cold to the touch. Nobody was more uninterested in life than a resident of Macrosanti.

Mordecai looked at Ellie, her eyes red and puffy and her nose running. Since birth, this must have been the only time she had cried with such passion. Crying was liberating. It was the acceptance of pain or misery or even happiness—but Mordecai couldn't blame her. It was almost impossible for her to liberate herself, he thought. How could she remove her shackles if she didn't know she was wearing them?

They walked back toward the two patrollers at the end of the bridge. Before they reached them, Mordecai snuck the book into Ellie's pants' pocket.

"This will liberate you, Ellie," Mordecai whispered to her. "Please read it. It has already freed my mind, but I cannot go without you. We can't go unless you free yourself."

Ellie took Mordecai's hand and squeezed it.

One of the patrollers extended his arm and escorted Ellie back inside. The other gestured the same to Mordecai but he waved him off.

I don't need an escort. I already know my way.

Three Heartbeats

Three heartbeats were picked up on the sonar.

It's never three heartbeats.

Sometimes it's one, other times two for testing purposes, but never three.

Kendra tapped the screen sewn into her uniform to make sure the sonar was calibrated correctly.

It was.

Three heartbeats were picked up. It's *never* three. And Kendra had never seen three, nor was ever told that three still existed, but those three thumps emanating from her arm had a familiar residue to them.

"Three heartbeats means life," Lamisse said like a formal statement.

"Or death," Jodie joked from the other side of the street. She was hovering her mineral detector over a fallen signal tower. "But it's okay, nothing's gonna kill us. Angels live forever."

Nothing lives forever, Kendra said to herself. Nothing good at least. Nothing good lives forever, and bad seems to always stick around longer than it should.

"How far away is it?" Lamisse asked.

Kendra gave her a dissatisfied look, knowing that she could just check her sonar screen.

"You know there's one on your arm too, Lammie," Jodie called out to her.

Lamisse glanced at her arm. Her cheeks flushed with red from embarrassment. "Yeah, I knew that."

Kendra smirked. Both of them were rookies but Jodie must have paid more attention in boot camp.

"All those books you've been shoving in your head from training must've suffocated your common sense," Jodie giggled. Then she turned to Kendra, who hid her smile.

Kendra preferred her old teammates, but you can't do any excavation work when you're vaporized, so the department gave her new teammates.

Jodie was adventurous, risky, and naturally curious. Dark caverns, abandoned buildings, anything that screamed DO NOT ENTER, she would turn over every rock or piece of debris to make sure the whole place was excavated. Jodie embodied a firecracker, someone who could light up a sky of darkness, but couldn't tell you when her fuse was lit. She even came up with the idea of calling the team "Harley's Angels" and got custom-sewn patches on their uniforms. Harley was the name of Jodie's pitbull back home.

Lamisse was timid, shy, cautious. Sometimes clumsy but very smart. Kind of like a lamb. When Jodie first showed the team the new patches, Lammie was worried that wearing them violated some sort of unspoken uniform code. Jodie scoffed at this, told Lammie to chill out, and sewed the patch on her shoulder sleeve. Then she sewed one on Kendra's.

Kendra wasn't sure what gravitated her toward working the wrecked cities, looking for the remnants of old minerals and the remains of anything with a heartbeat.

Anything human.

Or anything with three heartbeats.

Not human.

And there lived the possibility of vaporization. But the possibility was slim, Kendra had been told in multiple briefings. They had all been wiped out, a general with decorated badges covering his chest had assured her—yet Kendra's team had no problem being reduced to a microscopic heap of molecules. She hadn't seen the general since.

Even though vaporization was a possibility, you didn't believe it could happen to you. Vaporization didn't have human dimensions and it didn't deter you from living or working or having opinions. An archeologist didn't believe a tyrannosaurus would sprout from the soil and eat her team just as a weatherman didn't believe a tornado would form in his living room and whisk him up in the air and hurl him thousands of yards away. The thought of vaporization didn't deter one from doing anything, especially Kendra, until it took her team. Dare she say, her friends. And like dixie cups pulled from a tube next to a water jug, Kendra's friends had been replaced with a new team.

***

The Angels walked through the wrecked city, the three heartbeats thumping steadily on Kendra's arm.

"Three sinoatrial nodes in the heart," Lammie said to Kendra like she was reading from a textbook. "That's why it beats like that. And it can keep beating on its own for weeks after its host body dies."

Maybe Lammie had paid attention in boot camp, Kendra thought. Or maybe she just wanted to make small talk because she was nervous. Nervous about being in the field without the protection of sitting in a chair enclosed between four walls. Something about Lammie's nervousness gave her a sense of familiarity—one she couldn't figure out.

They finally reached the main road of the city, which was ruptured and wrecked. Cracked asphalt and mutilated cars patterned the road and vines held the decrepit buildings in a vice grip. In front of them stood one of the buildings, an old place of work made entirely of glass windows, most of which were now shattered or covered in vines. According to sonar, the heartbeats were pulsating from inside. Jodie started to walk in before Kendra put a hand on her shoulder.

"Your crazy ass wants to go see what has three heartbeats?"

Jodie smirked. "And you don't? I wanna get samples of its teeth. I bet the remains are glorious."

"If they even are remains."

"They *are* remains. They've all been wiped out."

Kendra could hear the words coming from the general's lips, followed by the jiggling of the badges on his uniform when she started screaming at him with hot tears welling out of her eyes. *When I cried, he loved to slam the table, Kendra remembered.*

"It's not part of the mission," Kendra reminded Jodie. "We're just here to confirm the location of the heartbeats. Then our autotrucks—"

"—will send in the rest of the excavation force, I know, I know. But three heartbeats. That's cool as hell."

"And dangerous as hell. We can't risk it."

"We need to at least verify the remains."

Kendra looked over at Lammie, who stood shyly like a child lost in a large crowd. Lammie glanced across the street at an old bike laying on the ground, rusted with a missing handle. She probably wanted to study it for old minerals but decided against it. She wouldn't say anything, Kendra knew that.

"Fine. But quickly. I'll go first."

Jodie put a fist in her open palm and faced Kendra.

"Rock, paper, scissors for it."

Kendra raised an eyebrow. "I'm sorry, I forgot to bring my toddler to work with me. Gonna have to wait to play another time."

Jodie frowned and they all entered the building—Kendra first, then Jodie with disapproval, followed by Lammie anxiously straggling behind.

The inside was just as wasted as the outside. Exposed copper wiring hung from the walls. Fluorescent panels flickered with light from above. Cement and other debris coated the carpeted floor.

Jodie unholstered her pistol.

"You don't need that," Kendra scolded her.

"You don't need it 'til you need it." Jodie grinned at her while loading a fresh round of bullets.

Kendra rolled her eyes, knowing she didn't have time to argue and started looking around the lobby, as did the rest of the team. Kendra found a plaque coated in a layer of dust near an elevator.

"Six floors. We don't have enough time to check all of them and make it back to the drop point."

"Fine, we'll each take two floors," Jodie proposed.

"We don't break from the group," Kendra said sternly.

"We'll be fine."

"You don't know that."

"We'll be *fiiiine*," Jodie said slowly.

Kendra had heard the familiar words before. They danced in her ears with a pulsating screech. Those familiar words. Harmless yet so harmful. One minute someone says them, the next minute they're vaporized.

"I can't have the team split."

"Look, I know we're rookies, but eventually you're gonna have to take that giant stick out of your ass and let us go solo. I think the four excavations we already did were enough 'team bonding.' " Jodie made air quotes with her fingers.

"She's right," Lammie chimed in from behind. "All rookie excavators are equipped to go solo so long as they rendezvous with the rest of the team by daybreak."

Lammie sounded like she was reciting the Official Excavator's Manual, which she probably was. Common sense may have been suffocated in her head but books had more air than they could breathe.

"If you let us split up," Jodie added. "Then our excavations won't take so long."

"I'm not letting the team split up."

"But then it'll take hours—"

"I don't care."

"Fine!" Jodie burst out. She tapped the up arrow button next to the elevator which lit up in a revolting orange color. She added dryly, "Let's see if this elevator at least works."

The ceiling sang with the whirring of gears and motors and suspension ropes until the elevator doors parted. The walls of the elevator car were peeling. The handrails rusted. The floor was a nauseous maroon, as if someone had been stabbed repeatedly until they became a puddle, which nobody bothered to mop up. Kendra rested her arm on a handrail, then removed it quickly to reveal a black stain on her palm.

"This place ought to be firebombed," Jodie said.

"Then we wouldn't be able to find the remains," Lammie mentioned.

"We find the remains, then we firebomb."

"Nobody is firebombing anything," Kendra said sternly.

Jodie nudged Kendra in the side. "Oh, c'mon. You know it'd be cool."

It would be cool.

The elevator doors opened to the second floor, a space of what used to be lines of desks and computer monitors, all smashed and broken. Kendra stepped out first, unhooked her interline camera, and started recording.

"Log number sixteen," she narrated. She looked at her forearm. "Three heartbeats still registering on the sonar, now showing closer to proximity."

From behind, as if waiting to creep up on her, she heard a loud ding. Kendra turned around to catch a glimpse of Jodie's smirk and Lammie's worried face as Jodie pulled her back before the elevator door closed on them both. Kendra ran to the door and banged on it.

"You're absolutely psychotic!" she shouted. "We can't afford to split up the team!"

"Don't worry," she could faintly hear Jodie's ascending voice. "We'll meet when we're done!"

Kendra, exasperated and in a blanket of sweat, put her hand over her chest, which throbbed so intensely one could mistake it for three heartbeats.

***

Kendra tried to pull her worried face into a professional, tempered one, but the ridges near her eyebrows refused to budge. She moved fiercely through the floor scattered with broken office equipment and cement chunks and found a door to the stairwell around the corner. Her steps were a vibrating thump which echoed through the stairwell like smoke rising up a chimney.

"Get down here!" Kendra shouted, her words echoing in the stairwell. No response. She was breathing violently through her nose. Her face heated like a stove.

Why is this happening again?

Even though those words sprouted in her head, she could not recall the remembered imagery of what happened before. She knew it was there in her head like one knows that muscles and nerves and bone rest under the skin of their hands.

While running up the stairwell, she jiggled the handles of five doors, all of them refused the budge until the sixth let her through.

Jodie would go to the sixth floor. Height compounds the danger which would compound the intrigue Jodie would have in it. Even if we had split up the floors, as she had proposed, she would have taken the highest one. Lammie wouldn't object. Jodie would've convinced her with some fabricated lie about how the remains are actually richer in old minerals the higher up they decompose. Even though Lammie would have never heard that in boot camp, she would have believed it.

The door let her through a narrow corridor with a ceiling of fluorescent panels, all of them out except for a few that twitched with light.

"Can you hear me?" Kendra shouted down the corridor.

The fluorescent panel twitched in response, as did her arm, which thumped with three heartbeats.

Kendra started walking with caution.

She took three corners until she saw a door, which opened to a custodial closet. She slammed the door but not before getting a whiff of chemicals.

A gunshot rang out at the end of the corridor.

"*Jodie*," she shouted. Jodie didn't say anything back. Only the echo of the gunshot lingered.

Kendra ran as fast as she could down the corridor, almost tripping over a loose chunk of cement until the corridor opened up into a spacious office with cracked walls and exposed pipes. A few chairs surrounded a rusted conference room table, surrounded by walls of glass. One wall was shattered completely.

Kendra heard her mom in her head.

"*God gave everyone two eyes: one to see love and one to see fear. But we get ourselves entangled when we use both eyes to only see one thing.*"

Kendra didn't remember anything else her mom said, and she wasn't sure why those words were so clear in her head. It wasn't even a particularly good quote, but it was all Kendra could think about as she paced quietly around the large room of scattered debris and exposed wiring.

"Jodie? Lammie?" she called out. "Can you hear me?"

The only response was a breeze that crept through an open window, and it ran a chill down her spine. The three heartbeats thumped on her arm. The gunshot still rang faintly in her ears, like tiny pebbles shaking inside a steel barrel.

Kendra heard her mom again.

"You need to tend to your own roots before you can blossom."

A faint cry for help came from the other side of the building.

Kendra rushed through a door and down a narrow corridor with an unpleasantly low ceiling. The light panels above twitched. Insulation seeped out from the walls. Pipes and vents were exposed. Crumbled plasterboard and drywall littered the floor. Another gunshot rang from behind a large steel door at the end of the corridor.

***

Kendra had heard of the creatures in briefings before she was sent into the ruined cities.

Heard about the virus and eventually about the three heartbeats.

Heard about the mass executions and mandatory quarantines.

Heard about the vaporizations—which rarely happened now, the general had assured her.

But Kendra had never seen a creature in the flesh. Never smelled its breath or felt its skin. But after carefully opening the heavy steel door at the end of the corridor, she didn't have to imagine anymore. Neither did Lammie, whose neck was being sucked on by one of the creatures.

"Get your filthy teeth away from her," Jodie was shrieking at the creature, aiming her pistol at its head. Its teeth, sharp and serrated like some prehistoric carnivore, gently penetrated the side of Lammie's neck, like pins poking into a cushion. It breathed a smokey breath. Its irises, surrounded by the rounded whites of its eyes, glared at the barrel of Jodie's pistol. Its hands—five mutilated appendages, discolored with pulsating white veins—were wrapped around Lammie's torso. It growled. Two arms, two legs, a head of hair, discolored, wearing a pair of torn pants and a t-shirt. This was no creature.

Lammie's eyes were frightened and dilated. She didn't move a muscle. Neither did Jodie, until she noticed Kendra staring at her.

"I have the shot. I won't hit her."

There were two bullet holes in the windows. Warning shots, Kendra thought.

"Don't you even think of putting your finger near that trigger."

Jodie cocked the pistol. The creature growled.

"I *won't* hit her."

"Don't you dare."

"It's infected. We need to put it down."

Lammie let out a blood-chilling scream as the creature started to sink its teeth deeper into her neck.

"Hey, hey!" Jodie yelled at the creature, gripping her pistol. "Get those fucking teeth of yours away from her."

The creature retracted a bit. Lammie's neck dripped with blood from the holes.

"You're not shooting anything with her in your line of fire."

"This thing is gonna infect the entire city if we let it go."

"You're going to kill her."

"*I won't hit her!*"

"No, she's right," Lammie mumbled while the creature's heavy arms constricted her chest. She started crying. The tears flowed down her cheeks.

"It's okay," she breathed. "We have to neutralize the infection. I'm probably already infected. They're gonna vaporize me, anyway."

"We don't know that!" Kendra cried out. She had a flash of her teammates' faces painted in horror as they banged on the glass window until their hands and fingers and everything else that made them exist was reduced to nothing.

The creature brought its teeth closer to Lammie's neck before Jodie took a step forward, pistol aimed at its head, and yelled, "Keep those fucking teeth away!"

"It's not going to listen," Lammie wailed. "You need to take the shot."

"You're gonna kill her!" Kendra howled.

Jodie slipped her finger in the trigger guard and rested her finger on the trigger. "There's no other option."

"There's always another option. Don't do this!"

Kendra started to walk toward Jodie. The creature growled. Jodie's eyes widened.

"Kendra, stop. Don't do this. You're going to start—"

"There's always another option!"

Serrated teeth flared out.

"Get back!"

Kendra lunged.

"There's always another option!"

The creature sank its teeth deep into Lammie, whose cries were muffled by the gunshot. Kendra tackled Jodie to the cold concrete floor. Her arm thumped in pain. Her nose leaked blood. It felt like time had stopped. Kendra screamed herself sick into a void until a blanket of white covered her vision.

***

A panel of light above blinded her. The hardness of the floor suddenly became soft, as if a sack of feathers had appeared below her. As she laid on her back, sitting atop that sack of feathers, Kendra realized that her pain had subsided.

The blood had disappeared.

Her arm had stopped thumping.

The sonar screen was gone, as was her whole uniform. It was replaced with a long white gown—the same as the gowns of the people surrounding her.

She tried to speak but a plastic tube snaked down her throat and pushed something into her chest. Her body didn't feel pain but it also didn't feel anything else. Her fingers refused to twitch despite her brain's attempt to move them. Her legs remained stiff. Her neck felt as if it was screwed in position. She could blink, and that was about it.

When she finally blinked, which took a few seconds, a screen sitting on a skinny pole started registering numbers and graphs. The group of people in the long white gowns chatted amongst themselves as if she had been asleep for a long time and had just woken up. There were four of them until a fifth, an old and distinguished-looking man with wireframe glasses, walked into the room.

The chatting stopped.

"Mental trauma patient KS-2591," one of the white gowns said to the distinguished man. He was a young, pencil-thin man holding a tablet.

"A Kendra Burkhardt," he added, gesturing to Kendra's body lying like deadwood on the table.

"*Oo-hee*," Kendra mumbled, the tube blocking her words. "*Aahm-hee. Ayre are ay? I eed oo eind em.*"

"Patient showed signs of dissociative behavior, including selective mutism and self-harm." He flicked his finger over the tablet as if to turn a digital page. "Patient's seventeenth round of immersive psychotherapy was administered today at seven-twenty-four AM."

The distinguished man gave a dissatisfied look. Kendra could read the letters stitched on his white gown. His name was Lewis Kridan.

"And?" Kridan said.

The man with the tablet cleared his throat. "And—we were waiting for you to assess the results."

He handed the tablet over to Kridan, who adjusted his wire-frame glasses and started reading.

"*Oo-hee*," Kendra gargled. "*Aahm-hee.*"

Kridan then glanced at the monitor with the numbers and graphs, then back to the tablet. Then to Kendra.

"*Oo-hee. Aahm-hee.*"

He shook his head.

"Round seventeen yielded no positive results. Patient KS-2591 is far from psychological recovery. Marcus, you can stop the methohexital and the succinylcholine."

Marcus, a thin-shouldered man with dark stubble, adjusted one of the half dozen fluid bags hanging over Kendra's head. She was able to slowly move parts of her body followed immediately by a nasty headache. The pain had come back. Then she remembered what had happened.

"Hello Kendra," Kridan said. "Do you know where you are?"

The light panels above were blinding, like they were flashlights shining right into her retinas.

"*Oo-hee,*" Kendra croaked. "*Aahm-hee. Ay eed ou—*"

"Do you know where you are, Kendra?" Kridan asked again.

"*Oo-hee. Aahm-hee. Ay—*"

"Do you remember the accident?" he asked. "Do you see their faces?"

"*Oo-hee. Aahm-hee.*"

"They don't exist, Kendra. Do you know where you are?"

"*Oo-hee.*"

"Do you know where you are, Kendra?"

"*Aahm-hee.*"

Kridan gestured for one of the white gowns to cart Kendra's bed down a brightly lit hall and into another room, which must have been her room because there was a bouquet of colorful balloons with her name plastered on the largest one.

The medication started to wear off, and she had forgotten the names and where her brain had just been. Kendra felt she had been submerged under water and had just risen to the top to gasp for air. The memories started to flood in, and so did the realization of where she was and what her life really was. Then the misery came back.

Kendra's neck felt it had been unscrewed and could look to the side. On her left was a large glass window, where she could see Kridan consoling her mother. She was in tears.

A few hours later, Kendra's mother entered the room. She sat on a stool by her bedside and took a gentle grip of her limp hand. Her hands were warm.

"How are you doing, sweetheart?" she softly asked.

Kendra sat there mute, as she always did. The TV in the corner played at low volume, someone on some show was trying to win money. Her mother kept stroking her hand. "He still hasn't called or even responded to any of my letters," she said. "I do hope he's taking care of her, she's such a wonderful child."

Kendra said nothing. Her eyes stared intently at the wall.

Kridan came into the room.

"We need to administer another round," he gently mentioned to Kendra's mother. "Your daughter showed little to no psychological improvement in the simulated reality. She still has deep memories of her two friends and what happened to them. They kept creeping into the environment."

She gave him a worried look.

"I don't understand. Why do we have to do this so many times?"

Kridan adjusted his glasses. "Like I said before Mrs. Burkhardt, The immersions light up areas of her brain that hold those traumatic experiences of her friends. When they light up, we can find them and remove them properly. But we have to be careful."

Kendra's eyes were sunken and her hair frizzed in a wild bushel. She was weak, like all the vital organs in her body were failing. Kendra's mom looked wistfully at her.

"Can you at least make her happy?" Kendra's mother asked hopefully. "I'm not fond of this specific immersion environment. Maybe if we—"

Kridan shook his head. "So far, this environment has minimized the negative results. With some adjustments, we might start to see results shift into positive. You must understand that what we are doing is quite experimental, and we need to make sure we are targeting the right parts of the brain or we can damage her forever. She can have paralysis, or go completely blind, or have permanent memory loss. It is in our best interest, Mrs. Burkhardt, that we be very careful with the experiment."

Kendra's mother pulled a cloth from her purse to wipe her eyes. Kridan gave her a consoling look.

"We have to do this delicately," he said. "Or else we risk changing a part of her brain that keeps her like this forever."

Kendra could now better understand the words Kridan was saying. She refused to say anything. Her heart oscillated between sadness and rage, not letting either emotion show itself.

Kendra's mother looked at her affectionately, caressing her hand.

"I don't want her to have the surgery," she said sternly. "I don't want you cutting into my daughter's head. If there's a chance at rehabilitation, then I'll sign the consent form."

Kridan nodded. "It may help to say something else to her. She may do better this time with the right words from you. It may light up the areas more accurately."

He left the room. Kendra's mother looked deep into her eyes. She gave a smile that could melt the ice in the coldest tundra. She took Kendra's hand into both of hers and whispered something in her ear, then she left the room.

In the entire psychiatric ward of bustling nurses, shuffling papers, and squeaking rubber-bottom shoes, there wasn't so much as a peep from Kendra's room. She lay in the hospital bed, uttering not a single word to anyone. She didn't eat or move, refusing to do either. Her body still had to function so she soiled her bed and the nurses had to force feed her soup. The nurses also came in to give her new pillows and sheets, sometimes even changing the channel on the little TV in the corner that stayed on all night, but Kendra never watched it. "It's a lovely day today," a nurse would say, but Kendra would just stare at a fixed point on the wall, not even blinking to acknowledge her.

Kendra had been, for many years, a speechless, spoiled vegetable, and her mother had no clue what to do with her. Diagnostic tests were run, exams were performed, x-rays, MRIs, CT scans, the elements of Kendra's vocal muscles were normal, intact and fully functional. She chose not to speak. Her mind wouldn't allow it. Trust between people had been severed and her fear of loss had been compounded to the point of dissociation with loss itself. That belief infected every crevice of her brain.

Kendra sat in that room, rotting away until a few of the white gowns came in and wheeled her to another room. It only took two hours of being off the medication for Kendra to remember the car. As she remembered, she was already being strapped up for another round.

A 1997 Toyota Corolla.

Blue.

A dent the size of a bowling ball on the side.

Stella wanted the car to match her eyes, Kendra remembered. Ashley said she should've gotten it in hot pink. Kendra didn't care about the color. She also remembered sitting in the front passenger seat because she was nervous about Stella's driving and wanted to be a second set of eyes.

That decision had spared her life.

"Patient ready for immersion," one of the coats said.

A circular device crowned her head and electrical nodes were placed on her forehead.

All Stella talked about was how excited she was to marry Edward. She wanted to move to Los Angeles with him, raise a family of beautiful children, and spend her days sitting by a pool shaded by palm trees. Stella wasn't the only person leaving their hometown. Ashley was moving to Wisconsin with her boyfriend at the end of the month. She had gotten into law school and her boyfriend landed a comfy job at a PR firm so they broke their lease and got the moving trucks ready. But before Stella would marry Edward and move to Los Angeles and before Ashley would be drowning in case studies under a faint light at the library, they wanted to have one last hurrah at their favorite bar. An impromptu bachelorette party for Stella and a going away party for both of them. And behind her smiles and laughter that night,

Kendra was bracing for the only two friends she had ever had to leave her all alone.

A monitor started beeping and showing charts and figures with rapidly changing numbers.

It was just a short drive home from the bar, Kendra remembered. And in that car that night, there was the rhythmic thumping of three heartbeats wrapped in a beautiful friendship. Three heartbeats that had given each other their love, their righteous innocence, their vulnerability.

"Go for methohexital," another coat said.

A needle slid into her arm.

Three heartbeats that had battled each other with passion and judgment but had loved and healed. Three heartbeats that had shelter within each other, where they had peace within themselves. And when that shelter was destroyed, reduced to rubble, Kendra ceased to be at peace, and her good would always be tortured by that bitter memory, one that built walls, closed doors, and fastened locks.

"Go for succinylcholine."

Another needle slid into her arm.

As the car tumbled off the highway, barrel-rolling with three bodies strapped in for dear life, it severed two of them, their wings extended wide, carrying them up into the clouds. Before they were lifted up, Kendra was able to see the beautiful eyes of her friends seconds before their eyelids closed completely and seconds before their souls would be lifted from the ground. That night, that awful night, left Kendra wingless and grounded forever.

"Go for immersion."

The electrical nodes buzzed and the monitor beeped. Kendra felt her body becoming weightless and her vision hazy. Then everything was black. A deep void of nothingness followed by a kaleidoscope of colors as Kendra felt she was being launched into some interstellar wormhole. Then the blackness came back, and the memories of her life slowly faded away like a fine mist in the sunlight.

Her hands suddenly gripped a mineral detector. Her feet were fitted with sturdy brown boots. Her body was wrapped in a heavy camouflage uniform. She walked through the wrecked city, cracked asphalt and mutilated cars patterned the road.

Kendra's arm started thumping. Three heartbeats were picked up on the sonar.

It's never three heartbeats.

Sometimes it's one or two, but *never* three.

"Three heartbeats means life," Lamisse said like a formal statement.

"Or death," Jodie joked at her. "But it's okay, Angels live forever."

Nothing lives forever, Kendra said to herself. Nothing good at least. Bad seems to always stick around longer than it should.

And like a soft lullaby tickling the inner ear, a gentle harmonic tone that could relax even the most restless child, her mother's words gently brought themselves to her ears.

"Your wings were never taken." Her soft voice spoke in her head. *"You've just kept them hidden. You've hidden them long enough. Show the world what a beautiful angel you are."*

And as the three of them walked through the ruined city, the three heartbeats pounding on Kendra's arm, she thought how nice it would be for her to spread her wings so that they may lift her up into the clouds to live with the rest of the angels.

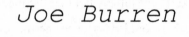
Joe Burren

Look:

Joe Burren makes $325,000 a year.

He also beat his wife to a pulp.

Joe lives in Sammamish, Washington. The violent crime rate in Sammamish is 93% lower than the national average. Joe keeps his garage door unlocked so the neighbor's kid can get the lawnmower to cut his grass. Joe pays the neighbor's kid $30 a week to do this. Before, he paid no one. Joe was used to doing manual labor on his own, but recently he thought it'd be good to finally talk to other people. Joe liked the neighbor's kid. He also liked his neighbors. They kept to themselves, never caused a ruckus with the HOA, and never told him what he could or couldn't put in front of his house.

Joe had gone over to their place for dinner one night. They served him broccoli chicken casserole. It was a very good meal, and Joe hadn't had a home-cooked meal in a long time. The neighbors moaned about their son, who always complained about not having enough allowance to buy candy and video games, so Joe proposed that he could start mowing his lawn. The neighbors thought it was a splendid idea, and the money was plenty for the kid to go buy all the candy and video games he wanted.

Look:

Joe Burren makes $325,000 a year.

He also beat his wife to a pulp.

Joe was born three pounds too big so his mother's belly was cut open to get him out. Joe didn't choose to be that big, but he was big nonetheless, and the doctors could only get him out with a scalpel.

After that, Joe's mom aged like goat cheese. Varicose veins and weight problems and diabetes. She blamed Joe for all of it, enviously watching him grow into his perfectly capable body wrapped in a layer of taintless skin while her body decayed like an expired apple.

Joe didn't have a good relationship with his mom as she started to decompose, but she was, nonetheless, an adequate mother. Meals were cooked, clothes were cleaned, beds were made, and cuts were covered with bandaids (accompanied by an emotionless stare and a gutting comment about Joe's clumsiness).

Then Joe's mom passed on one night while she was sitting in her rocking chair. Two days prior, Joe and his kindergarten classmates were making Mother's Day cards. Joe's letter was sitting in his cubby, waiting for a few flower stickers to be added to the corners as the rocking chair ceased to rock and the paramedics took his mom away on a gurney.

Joe went to live with his Aunt Rita in Cottage Lake since he didn't have a dad around. Joe wished he had met his dad, but his Aunt Rita was quite alright. Her house was considerably bigger and she took care of Joe just like his Mom did. Meals were still cooked, clothes were still cleaned, beds were still made, and cuts were still covered with bandaids. It was better than an orphanage, Joe thought.

Joe had crooked teeth for most of his childhood because braces were too expensive. He also had a really big nose and the other kids made fun of it. When a kid in class coughed, they'd say it was because Joe was breathing up all the air and that there wasn't enough for everyone else to breathe. Joe thought this was funny for two days—it lasted for about four years.

Joe's childhood was unremarkable and scattered with half-baked memories that Joe had trouble recalling. He only remembered how the kids called him names because of his nose—in his opinion, his nose wasn't actually that big. Everyone else just had tiny little sniffers.

When Joe got to high school, he had grown to a remarkable six feet and two inches. He was a silent giant, rarely speaking and often keeping to himself. He liked shop class and painting and that was about it.

Joe only had two friends from high school. The first was Neil, who went on to work in corporate finance, which Joe had no interest in listening to when he spoke about it. The other was Robby, who ended up moving to Brazil to work for a humanitarian project. He died in a car crash two years later.

By his junior year, he had only kissed one girl before dating Amy Brown. Amy Brown kissed really well and always smelled of strawberries. They met in English class. They were paired up to do a group project on the importance of poetry. Joe went over to her place to practice their presentation and before they could finish their dry run, they were already playing tonsil tennis.

They dated for a few months—picnics at the park, walking around the mall, kissing in the back row of movie theaters. Amy asked Joe if he had ever had sex and he said no. Amy then asked if he'd want to have sex with her, but Joe told her no because he wasn't ready. Joe loved Amy, then liked her, then felt her to be tolerable until he felt complete disinterest toward her, so when the cute girl in shop class who always wore a beanie and ripped jeans asked him if he wanted to help her finish her wooden coat rack after school, he felt he couldn't say anything but yes.

This broke Amy's heart, and eventually Joe's.

Look:

Joe Burren makes $325,000 a year.

He also beat his wife to a pulp.

Joe wanted to go to college, but the high school guidance counselor had only raised eyebrows for him. He would have to get his grades up, do some volunteer work, or even play a sport to put on the resume. Being the second tallest person in his class and having a firm disdain for textbooks and exams, Joe joined the basketball team. He wasn't athletic, agile, or fast. He didn't even have good hand-eye coordination. During games, he would usually just stand still in the paint like a large tree and grab the balls that didn't go into the hoop with his two long arm-branches and put them back in. Sometimes, he would throw the ball to the shorter, quicker players so they could put the ball in the hoop. His coach told him that he should play in college, but Joe had no interest in doing such a thing.

Joe applied to three colleges.

He got into one.

It was in eastern Washington. College classes made no sense to him, as they had made no sense when he was in high school. Cram information into your head and then regurgitate it on a piece of paper. He couldn't understand why someone would memorize information just for arbitrary letters. High school was mandatory, Joe's Aunt Rita had told him, but she never said anything about college, so he spent just three months there before dropping out and moving back in with her in Cottage Lake.

Joe's Aunt Rita was ambivalent about Joe living back home with her after college. Joe was tidy and didn't cause any trouble. He didn't abuse drugs or have frequent run-ins with the police. His room was in the basement and they had ample space between each other in the house. But his Aunt Rita had one rule for Joe if he wanted to stay.

He'd have to get a job.

Look:

Joe Burren makes $325,000 a year.

He also beat his wife to a pulp.

Joe's first gig was flipping burgers at Scooter's. He was paid as little as the government mandated Scooter's to pay him, which was enough to pay the rent on a dumpster if he ever chose to live in one. On his second day at Scooter's, he burned a patty so badly, a customer approached the counter and slammed the burger to the ground, splaying its guts on the tiled floor. Joe was fired three weeks into the gig because he was late for his morning shift multiple times because he was having night terrors about his mother and couldn't sleep the night before. Later in life, Joe went to a therapist about his mother and eventually the night terrors went away.

He was then hired at a software company as a sales rep. He was put in a cubicle with a clackety keyboard and a monitor and a stapler that never seemed to work. On his first day, he filled out paperwork. On his second day, his boss dropped a stack of business cards on his desk and told him to start dialing. On his third day, he quit. Joe wasn't a born salesman and bothering people over the phone wasn't something he was interested in doing.

Joe found a job advertisement for a warehouse order selector at Production Food Corp. The job would involve operating pallet jacks and forklifts and organizing products to be loaded onto trucks, all while following food safety protocols. The pay was enough, the hours were good, and there was no college degree or previous warehouse experience required. There was also minimal human interaction, which Joe liked. He went through two interviews, one with the warehouse manager and one with another warehouse order selector (both of whom talked in a straightforward manner), and after they called him to tell him he got the job, he moved to Samammish and worked there for the next twenty years.

Look:

Joe Burren makes $325,000 a year.

He also beat his wife to a pulp.

Over the years, Joe came to the realization that he didn't want many of the things other people wanted. Joe didn't like to drink because it made him sick, so he stopped drinking. Joe also realized that he didn't like going out anymore, so he stopped doing that, too. Joe didn't like to spend money lavishly so he kept his wallet shut. He wanted to save his money for his future children, so he didn't go out to nice dinners or parties or events. Joe also avoided small talk as much as he could. He saw no use for it. He knew what the weather was, had no interest in other people's jobs, and yes, everyone hates traffic. He felt that he didn't need to blabber on about everything.

Joe liked to work, and outside of working in the warehouse, he developed a passion for woodworking and carpentry. Instead of buying new shelves and bookcases, he built them himself. He bought different types of wrenches, screwdrivers, hammers, and power drills. To save money, he would go to second-hand stores and garage sales to buy the tools at cheaper prices. He wanted to build his own shed, but there was no room in his apartment for such a thing so he kept all his tools in a small closet.

Joe was considerably alone, isolated from everyone else, but he was content. All of Joe's tools were his friends because they made sense. They had an objective purpose. The hammer to hammer in nails, and so on—but content was different than happy or fulfilled, and Joe would realize this later in life.

Look:

Joe Burren makes $325,000 a year.

He also beat his wife to a pulp.

Two days prior to meeting Sylvia, and fifteen years prior to almost punching the mortician for trying to oversell him on an expensive casket, Joe got a call from his boss, asking him if he could volunteer at the Haven Animal Sanctuary for the company's annual day of giving back. At least two employees from each warehouse were required, and Otto, one of Joe's co-workers, had come down with a nasty flu. Joe took his place and volunteered that day.

It was on a Saturday, which Joe usually reserved for walking around the nearby pond or building something with his tools but on this Saturday, he was brushing cows, scooping poop in pig pens, and feeding goats. Joe didn't mind getting dirty (as long as it was sawdust or grease or oil), but he did mind all the employees at Haven who constantly tried to talk to him about their love and support for animals and how he could contribute so much if he volunteered just once a month for a few hours. It was as if Jesus came back from the dead in the form of a cow and spoke nonsense to these hollow-heads, Joe thought as he scattered feed to a group of goats.

But then he saw her thick black hair, sitting on her shoulders elegantly, and when he got closer, he could see her beautiful blue-green eyes, flecked with gold and enclosed in a dark outer ring. When Joe first saw her, she was feeding a group of parrots. One of them was perched on her shoulder. Joe hated small talk more than anything but talking with Sylvia was anything but small. She had been an employee at Haven for five years (they called themselves team members), and had been working with animals, specifically birds, for over a decade. She gushed with passion about the parrots and the finches and everything else with wings, calling each of them beautiful and "part of the Haven family." She glittered with remarkable beauty, even though she was wearing baggy cargo pants and a beige collared shirt with the Haven logo stitched on the chest, and there was nothing else he wanted to do that day than to just talk to her.

Before he left the sanctuary, one of the Haven team members asked Joe if he would be interested in volunteering once a month.

Joe said yes, but only if he could come once a week instead.

Look:

Joe Burren makes $325,000 a year.

He also beat his wife to a pulp.

Joe waited three months to ask Sylvia out on a first date. At the future dinner parties Sylvia and Joe went to (Joe was more or less dragged by Sylvia to these parties), Sylvia joked about how long he took to ask her out. "I could have turned to stone by the time you'd ask me out," she'd say with an effervescent laugh and a shoulder rub. After the first date, they went on a second, then a third, and many more after that. By the fourth date, Joe had already started calling her Silvy, which she liked very much.

All the things Joe decided to not do anymore he was doing with Silvy. They went out to dinner, parties, shows, and movies. Joe didn't like small talk, didn't like talking with people, didn't like parties, but he loved Silvy, so he loved everything he did with her. One of the most memorable events was a Halloween party. Silvy dressed up as Maggie Fitzgerald from her favorite movie, Million

Dollar Baby, sporting a silk green robe, boxing gloves, and some makeup to give herself a black eye. Joe went as a mechanic, wearing a flannel from his closet and his utility belt of second-hand tools. It was also memorable because it was the first time they got into a fight that led to Silvy leaving the party early with eyes filled with wet tears. Joe didn't remember what the fight was even about, just that he'd never seen Silvy so upset at him.

Look:

Joe Burren makes $325,000 a year.

He also beat his wife to a pulp.

But they loved each other very much and Joe understood that fights were something every couple had to deal with, but that didn't make them any more desirable.

After some time, they bought a small house together. It was big enough to raise children, close enough to Haven and the warehouse, and the backyard had ample space for Joe to build a woodshed. He built it two weeks after signing the deed.

The backyard was also home to an old tree that Silvy refused to let Joe cut down as it would make a beautiful home for a family of birds, which she was right about since only after a few weeks, a family of them moved in.

Joe noticed how much Silvy loved those birds. She would sit outside all day next to the old tree in the backyard, watching them jerk their heads around, looking for worms, flaring their wings out to attract mates, grooming themselves with their beaks. Joe had no love for birds, but he loved Silvy, so he built them a birdhouse and nailed it to the old tree. More birds came, and Joe kept making larger, more complex houses for them. Silvy now spent twice as much time with them outside, making sure each of them got her attention. Joe only went outside to put up a new birdhouse.

Nothing more, nothing less.

Look:
Joe Burren makes $325,000 a year.
He also beat his wife to a pulp.

Silvy had always told Joe that there was nothing on this earth she loved more than him, and that he should really take care of his health. Joe's favorite appliance in their house was the microwave, and Joe had no time to make meals with healthy ingredients. Why not just buy the frozen meals and microwave them? It saves time and cooking is messy and unnecessary.

Silvy disagreed and started shopping at the local supermarket that Joe despised, the one where all the products were organic, gluten-free, Non-GMO with no artificial flavors or colors or preservatives, and the food cost twice as much as the food at the grocery store in the town square.

She started making healthier meals for Joe, packing his work lunches in little plastic containers with tiny handwritten notes she taped to the bottom so that Joe would have to eat the whole container of food to read them. If Joe couldn't tell her what her note said, she'd be awfully mad at him, and Joe never wanted to make her mad, so he always finished his lunch, made with organic, gluten-free, Non-GMO ingredients, and thanked her for the note when he got home from work.

Silvy also made sure Joe was treated right. Over the twenty years Joe had worked at Production Food Corp, he had never asked once for a promotion or a salary increase. He never took a vacation or a sick day. He never made excuses about the working conditions. Joe was the kind of guy to put his head down and make the best of what was around him. Corporate just gave him a standard 3% raise each year to keep up with inflation. Silvy told Joe that he should go to his boss and ask for a raise, that he deserved the higher salary for his loyalty and hard work. Also, the extra money would be good for when they decided to have children, so Joe went into work and asked his boss for a raise. They raised his salary by 20%, from $65,000 to $78,000.

Even with the raise, Joe and Silvy didn't have a lot of money. As fulfilling as Silvy's job was, Haven didn't pay like Wall Street. When Joe first met Silvy, she lived with three other girls, sleeping on a futon in a shared room with another girl who was also sleeping on a futon. Her apartment had a wood finish and a lot of her appliances were old and made of plastic or aluminum and a light bulb was always burnt out.

They got by with what they had, and both of them decided to be more frugal. Silvy's only expensive guilty pleasure was clothes, and she agreed to cut back on shopping. Joe didn't have any guilty pleasures for as long as he could remember. Anytime Joe bought anything lavish or luxurious, it was for Silvy, and only Silvy. And one of those lavish purchases was a white gold wedding ring that wrapped beautifully around her delicate finger.

They got married at a small chapel in Sammamish with only a few dozen people, then honeymooned seven years later in Australia when they could finally afford it. Australia had beautiful wildlife, and it was somewhere Silvy always dreamed of visiting, so Joe saved as much as he could for them to go.

Some days are just magical, Joe thought, like when he and Silvy lay together on the Australian beach under a cabana, watching the waves glide into the sandy shore, and Silvy, looking at Joe with those same blue-green eyes, flecked with gold and enclosed in a dark outer ring, told him that she wanted a family. And Joe had finally realized that content was different than happy or fulfilled because he wasn't just content anymore. He was happy. He was fulfilled.

Look:

Joe Burren makes $325,000 a year.

He also beat his wife to a pulp.

Family was something tender to Joe. Not having a father made him want to be a better father to his eventual son or daughter. He was also excited to build the crib.

Some days are just magical, like the day Silvy told Joe, with her delicate hands cradled in his, that she wanted to have a family, and some days are just brutal, agonizing, painful. But to everyone and everything else, they're just days. Numbers on a calendar. And those brutal days come and go as they please. They ebb and flow with no natural cadence. They come in your life, clumped between a group of average, normal days, making them almost unrecognizable. On one of these average days, Joe and Silvy were sitting on the couch, wrapped in blankets, watching TV on the wooden stand Joe built for it, and on another—Silvy had tubes going up her nose and into her arms, pumping her with medicine.

The medicine was supposed to cure her, Joe thought, which is why he was so angry when the nurses told him they had to take her body away. Joe went home that evening and sat on the couch, staring at the unfinished crib. He didn't move for hours. Then he put the unfinished crib in the dumpster.

Joe finally took a day off of work. He spent it walking around the pond. When he got home, he went into the backyard and saw that the family of birds had left the old tree. They had left with Silvy. He microwaved himself a bean burrito and fell asleep early. The next day, he went back to work.

Look:

Joe Burren makes $325,000 a year.

He also beat his wife to a pulp.

Joe wanted to punch the mortician for trying to oversell him on an expensive casket, a Belmont veneer with a cream interior. It wasn't the casket that made him so angry, it was the fact the he offered him a 20% discount if he bought it that day, and Joe couldn't help balling his fist and waving it at the mortician's face, enraged that he would offer a clearance deal on the vessel that would hold the body of his dead wife. Joe bought a casket from another mortician in Klahaine. Silvy was buried two days later in a mahogany casket with champagne velvet interior.

Joe kept going every week to the Haven Animal Sanctuary, feeding the birds, cleaning their exhibits, even on rare occasions giving brief talks to children about the birds, armed with all the facts Silvy had told him over the years. Joe didn't like talking with people, but he loved Silvy, and he knew she would have loved to talk to these kids about these wonderful creatures all day. So, he did it for her.

Joe cleaned out the tools in his shed. He realized there wasn't much more to build. Silvy usually had things for Joe to build—bookshelves, birdhouses, a new dinner table, a desk that sat in the basement for her to use when she studied for veterinary school. Now Silvy was gone, and so were the new things to build.

Joe was getting older, more frail, and if, god forbid, he got injured or fell off a ladder, there would be nobody to help him. He donated most of his tools. Some he gave to the Haven property managers, others went to local donation centers. The tools slowly left the shed until all the shelves were empty and the only thing left was the lingering smell of sawdust.

Joe kept himself locked away for some time, more than usual in fact. He felt like he couldn't speak to anyone. The pain he felt was undoubtedly harder than any pain anyone had ever felt in their life. He still went to work in Ellisville, an extra thirty-minute commute. Twice a week, he stopped at the grocery store in the town square on the way home, bought a few microwaveable meals with some milk and fruits, then spent the rest of the night reading or watching TV.

Joe and Silvy had met a few of their neighbors, but really it was Silvy who was the social bird with colorful wings, flourishing them to attract the attention of everyone, while Joe came along to social gatherings much like an awkward child or a man recently rehabilitated from an insane asylum—mute and unable to hold eye contact. Most of the neighbors knew Silvy, and only knew of Joe, but Joe felt he should stop wallowing in lonely sadness for the remainder of however much longer he had.

Thankfully, he had an opportunity.

The house across the street that had a for sale sign on it for the past few weeks was finally bought, and the nice couple that moved in knocked on Joe's door one day and invited him over for dinner. Joe obliged, and he went over to eat their delicious broccoli chicken casserole and met their kid who was more than happy to mow his lawn for a fair price.

Joe joined a support group of grieving spouses after two months of being alone. Joe didn't like small talk, but the other spouses in the group never did such a thing. Joe didn't like talking to other people, but there was something to be said about talking with someone with a shared tragedy that went beyond his general dislike. Grief is a familiar chord that is strummed in the hearts of every being that lives on this earth, and now more than ever, that cord wasn't just ringing in Joe's ears, it was thumping in his chest.

Look:

Joe Burren makes $325,000 a year.

He also beat his wife to a pulp.

As it does, life went on. Rain kept spattering the windows in the winter. The radio kept playing awful pop music. The forklifts kept whirring around the warehouse. Joe kept himself busy at the warehouse. The supervisors had him work more on product packaging and less operating forklifts and pallet jacks because of his age, which Joe disliked. At least if he got injured on the job, there would be others who could help—and a cash settlement.

Joe went to Cottage Lake one weekend to visit his Aunt Rita, who was now in an assisted living center. She gave Joe only wrinkled smiles and gargled words, but he spent as much time with her as he could.

Not a day went by when Joe didn't think of Silvy. He got as many photos of her framed as he could. He went to the print shop many times. He even knew the employees by their names, the things Silvy made Joe do. Joe didn't like talking to people who had nothing meaningful to say, but when it was about Silvy, suddenly they had everything to say.

In the backyard, a family of birds moved into the old tree. Joe wasn't sure what kind of birds they were. Silvy would know, he thought to himself. He brought food out for them once a week.

The days were getting better for Joe. The whirring of pallet jacks and forklifts kept his mind buzzing for most of the day. The group therapy helped him grieve. The neighbors gave him friendship. The birds in the old tree gave him responsibility. Volunteering at Haven gave him a connection to Silvy, but it was those brutal days clumped together with the average, normal ones that Joe feared the most.

On one average day when Joe got back from work, he flipped on the TV and saw a news report of protesters standing outside of Haven. They held signs and were shouting at the top of their lungs for the sanctuary to be shut down and bulldozed.

The protesters roared about the alleged mistreatment of animals at Haven. Joe couldn't believe these accusations. He could never envision Haven committing any of these awful crimes, so he decided to take a second day off work to drive to Haven and try to sort things out. As he drove on the gravel path leading to the entrance, the group of protesters, around forty of them, were holding different signs and wearing matching shirts.

Some of them were arguing with the Haven team members, others were holding cell phones in the air, video recording everything. Others were chanting a pre-rehearsed plea, for Haven to be shut down forever.

Joe got out of the car and tried to talk to the protesters. He approached a group of them to politely, trying to speak about his support for the animal sanctuary, saying they had been good to his wife, and had never seen them so much as lay a finger on a parrot in all the years his wife had worked there and in all of his hours of volunteering.

Joe tried to be polite with them. He tried to tell them all the good the sanctuary had done, how well they treated their animals and his wife, but they couldn't hear him, even though they stood so close to each other, their breaths colliding with each other.

The group was unmoved. Joe was shrouded from the cruelty—they suggested—that he would never see such horrific acts because of how damaging it would be to the sanctuary for such a committed volunteer like him to know about the abuse.

Joe could never believe something like this.

Look:

Joe Burren makes $325,000 a year.

He also beat his wife to a pulp.

You must understand that Joe was not a perfect person. He once stole a pen from a Walmart when he was fifteen. He once lied to the cops about drinking while driving when he was in college. He once forgot to bring a gift to his friend's wedding. He once tripped and broke a glass cabinet of merchandise in an antique shop in Wenatchee. He once had an old boss he hated so he pissed on his car's door handle on his lunch break. The worst thing Joe had ever done was cheating on Amy, which he regretted very much.

Joe was not a perfect person.

But understand that it's difficult to believe this, just like Joe didn't want to believe any of the accusations against

Haven. They were false accusations. They were lies, a way to tarnish the place that given him Silvy. The place that kept his connection with her alive after she passed on.

He slowly shed his politeness like an expired layer of skin and raised his voice to the group of protesters. They jawed back, and the cameras were all on Joe. He said some things he shouldn't have said. Awful things he could have never imagined saying before in his life.

He went home angry that day, almost angry enough to put a hole through the wall of his shed. By the next morning, his face was plastered online—videos of him available to anyone with a set of eyeballs. His words were branded online. Hateful and vile, they were labeled.

"How could someone support such an atrocious place?" one reporter said.

More online personalities chimed in, denouncing his words and giving their support to the protesters, demanding that Haven be bulldozed to rubble. One of the online personalities even made fun of Joe's nose.

Online activist groups scoured the internet to find information about Joe. They found his full name from Haven's website, listing their weekly volunteers. They traced that to an online work profile of a Joe Burren who was the senior vice president of a telecommunications company. One member of the forum linked a salary estimate for that job with the caption: *Making $325,000 a year, he probably doesn't give a rat's ass about the mistreatment of animals. Hell, he probably gets some sort of cut from bringing in exotic animals.*

Another member of the online forum surfaced a photo of Silvy, a picture she took of herself. Her eyes were puffy red as if she had just been crying and her eye was blackened to the color of tar. Joe saw that she was wearing a silk green robe and realized that it was a photo from the Hallowe'en party. The one where she dressed up as Maggie Fitzgerald. The one where they got into a fight. Joe couldn't bear to read more than four of the comments surrounding the picture.

"Just absolutely awful."

"This sick man beat his wife to a pulp."

"A disgusting, repulsive man."

And Joe couldn't understand that all these awful, inaccurate things people said about him were forever imprinted in the repository of information that everyone accessed all the time.

Look:

Joe Burren makes $325,000 a year.

He also socked his wife so hard in the face, it severed an optic nerve probably.

Joe tried to move on. He stopped volunteering at Haven. He couldn't show his face there again. His support group barred him from meetings, saying that Joe should not be allowed to grieve for a spouse he physically abused. The people in the warehouse gave him dirty looks and distanced themselves from him as much as they could. Joe's manager called him into his office a few days later, telling him that he wasn't going to fire Joe because of his loyalty, but that he should look for other places to work.

Joe felt that everything around him had crumbled, that he would need to leave this city that he called home. He could move to the countryside, find another job as a mechanic or a plumber or a dirty janitor, anywhere that would hire him. Anywhere that didn't know his name or knew that the things said about him were lies. It didn't matter at that point.

The neighbor's kid started to look at Joe in a way he never did before. One day, he asked for a raise and Joe said he couldn't pay him that much. Eventually he stopped coming to mow the lawn. He also stopped talking to Joe. So did the neighbors.

The days started to bleed away. Joe still went to work at the warehouse, ignoring the scrutinizing eyes like daggers from his coworkers. He read through magazines and searched online for jobs during his lunch break, even finding an opening as a janitor at a psychiatric ward out in the country. He still stopped at the grocery store on the way home to buy microwaveable meals (he even got a handful of glares there), and he still sat on his couch when he got home to watch TV for the rest of the night.

Joe stopped walking around the pond on Saturdays. He didn't like getting stared at by other people, imagining the things they were probably saying about him behind his back. On one weekend morning, he went outside to the backyard and saw that the family of birds had moved out and deserted his birdhouses. He went up to the old tree and put his hand on its thick truck, gliding his hands over its deep cracks and fissures. It was the only thing that didn't judge him, and he found solace in that. The birds would have stayed with Silvy, Joe lamented, but those awful, brutal days have to come with the normal, average ones. Or else life would just be normal. Life would just be content. Joe didn't know what kind of day today was. He felt like all the days had become awful and that the normal, even good days had ceased to exist.

And then Joe realized it was Sunday.

And there was no knock at his door.

So he walked to the shed and pulled the lawnmower out to start cutting the grass.

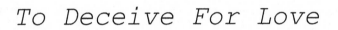

To Deceive For Love

Yesterday, I received an email from a Dan Smith at info@moh.gov.ss.

Subject: *You have an outstanding payment!!!*

While I waited for my coffee I started reading it.

Hi Ricardo, this is important information.

Okay, you have my attention.

For the last couple of months, I have been watching you :) About six months ago I gained access to your devices, which you use for internet browsing and I have been tracking your internet activities.

Oh no.

Here is the sequence of events: Some time ago I purchased access to email accounts from hackers It is quite simple to purchase such thing online.

I do remember reading about that somewhere.

I have easily managed to log in to your email account (ricardo7732@standardmail.com).

Oh no, that is my actual email.

I have already installed a Trojan virus to the operating systems of all the devices that you use to access your email. It was not really hard at all since you were followed many of the links from your inbox emails. Ingenious yet simple! Hahaha

He's toying with me! The revolting creature!

This software provides me with access to the microphone, video camera and keyboard of all your device. I have downloaded all your information, data, photos, web browsing history, etc. to my servers. I have access to all your messengers, social networks, emails, chat history and contacts list.

No, no, no, this can't be happening.

While gathering information about you, I have discovered that you are a big fan of adult websites.

Isn't everyone?

You really love visiting porn websites and watching exciting videos, while experiencing an enormous amount of pleasure.

I'm not sure what else you would do on those sites.

I have recorded a number of your dirty scenes and montaged a few videos, which show the way you masturbate and reach orgasms.

Oh.

If you have doubts, with a few clicks of my mouse all your videos will be shared to your friends, colleagues and relatives.

Not Grandma Shana!

I have also no issue at all making them available for public access. I guess you really don't want that to happen, considering the specificity of the videos you like to watch, (you perfectly know what I mean)—it will cause a true catastrophe for you.

He's right. I may have to leave the country. My hard drive is filthier than a drainage pipe.

Let's settle it this way:

Okay, I'm listening.

You transfer $1450 USD to me in bitcoin equivalent according to the exchange rate at the moment of funds transfer, and once the transfer is received, I will delete all this dirty stuff right away.

Well, you've forced my hand! I don't see any other way out of this quandary.

After that we will forget about each other. I also promise to deactivate and delete all the harmful software from your devices. Trust me, I keep my word.

Thank God. At least he's an honest man.

My bitcoin wallet ID is at the bottom of email. You have less than 48 hours from the moment you opened this email. Don't try to find me—it is absolutely pointless. All the cryptocurrency transactions are anonymous. * Don't try to—

The bitter taste of my coffee interrupted my reading.

"What the hell is this?" I shouted.

I held up the cup to her, standing there like a baby lamb in her yellow shirt of patterned daisies, gawking at me with those eyes. Her poor paralyzed soul.

"You have a fine brain in working order, don't you?"

"I'm sorry, I just—"

"Never mind. I'll drink it—just don't forget the sugar next time."

Dolly didn't say anything. Dolly wasn't her actual name, but I preferred to call her Dolly. She wasn't wearing the lipstick from the kit I bought her. She didn't even bother to tidy herself up today. Her lips, which should be a plush crimson red, were a cracked, faded pink. Her long auburn hair, which usually fell elegantly like silk, was frizzy and unkempt. Her eyes, which usually glittered like gemstones, stared at me with a bleak dullness. I was not prepared to see my poor pale child look so naturally boring like a flowerless forest. Had we lost the spark between us?

I took another sip.

"Don't worry," I said, comforting her with a strong arm on her bare, feeble shoulder. "It's alright."

Her cracked lips twitched into a curled smile.

"And the puppy?" she delicately asked.

Now she'd done it. I snapped at her. "Not *another* word of this getting-a-puppy nonsense, do you understand?"

Her smile recoiled into a frown. She nodded and left my study through the sturdy oak door. I continued reading the email.

Don't try to reinstall the OS on your devices or destroy them.

It is pointless as well to find my data, since all the videos have already been saved on remote servers.

*You don't need to worry that I won't be able to receive your funds transfer. Don't worry, I will see it right away, once you complete the transfer, since I continuously track all your activities. My Trojan virus has a remote-control feature, something like TeamViewer. * That I will not share your videos after you complete the funds transfer. Trust me, I have no intention to continue creating troubles in your life. If I really wanted that, I would have done it a long time ago!*

Well, if you promise to stop here, maybe we can grab a coffee or go play laser tag.

One more thing... Don't get caught in similar kind of situation again in future. My advice—keep changing all your passwords on a frequent basis.

With best regards,
Dan Smith.

After reading the email, I slugged back the sugarless coffee and called my tech wiz buddy, Kit. He owed me a favor, so I had him do his techy magic to pull a name and address for me. Only took the sonofabitch a few hours.

Donald Parker.
62115 East Maple Drive.

A four-hour drive, but it was on the way to Stenson Candi's World Famous Circus in Sunnyville (how I will rekindle this spark, my love!). I solidified a plan to go there this weekend with Dolly.

I had my buddy, Jarvis, (who also owed me a favor and happened to live only 40 minutes from Donald) set up some live feed cameras of Donald's house. This let me monitor his day to make sure he would be there when I arrived.

To my surprise, Donald had a lovely home—a nice craftsman design in a light oak color with a large front garage. It had a beautifully landscaped front yard with rows of lush green shrubbery, perfectly manicured, that lined the stone pathway to the door.

How lucrative it is to be a scammer! How profitable it must be to swindle and deceive people into giving you their riches. Does the crying and distress of his victims make him roll around in bed at night or does he sleep undisturbed like a hibernating bear? I wonder how much money he has pried away from the defenseless hands of the senile and technophobic. Enough to buy himself a very classy home, one bigger than mine at least!

After monitoring him for the three days leading up to the weekend, I realized this operation would be much easier than I thought. Donald lived quite the ordinary life. He left his home in an old silver Saturn S-Series (plate # A2HXW92) around eight o'clock in the morning and came back at one in the afternoon. He had only left his house twice after that at the hours of three and six o'clock. As long as I showed up after one o'clock, there was a good chance he would be home. Now all I had to do was decide between wood or aluminum.

***

The four-hour drive wasn't as bad as I thought. Granted, the drive was just an interlude leading to the inevitable rekindling of our love in the form of Stenson Candi's circus.

I parked on the street outside Donald's house and put on my hazard lights. It was two o'clock in the afternoon and the Saturn sat in the driveway. I knocked on the door and a plump young man in a striped shirt and skinny jeans cracked it open. He looked at me with suspicious eyes, wondering if he should let his guard down. This had to be Donald.

"Yes, can I help you?"

It appeared he didn't know what I looked like. I initiated an Oscar-worthy performance.

"Sir, I'm so sorry to bother you! I know it's such a pain but the battery in my car died and I don't have any cell service. Do you have a phone inside I could use to call a tow truck?"

He dumbly blinked a few times. "You have a cell phone?"

"I do. It's just not getting any service."

He lifted a suspicious eyebrow while I tried to peek through the slit of the door to see if anyone else was there. I couldn't see diddly squat.

"You mind if I take a look?" Donald asked.

"Not at all."

I handed him my cell phone. I had stripped the SIM card out of it earlier, so he fumbled around with some of the settings on the phone with a perplexed look on his face.

"This is odd," he said. "It looks like it's missing the SIM card. Do you have it?"

I scratched my head like a dimwit. "Oh, I'm not sure! I'm not a big gadget guy, I'm sorry. I just need to make a call and I'll get out of your hair."

And with the last breath of altruism he must've had in his body, he accepted and opened his door for me.

"You can use my cell phone," he said, walking into the living room. I gripped the handle of the aluminum bat that I had secretly placed behind a potted plant at the front door and followed him in.

He fumbled around a countertop looking for his cell phone, saying how he just had it in his hands and he felt silly that he couldn't remember where it was.

Not that he would ever remember after today.

He found it under a stack of loose paper, probably transaction reports of victims who fell prey to sending this crook their hard-earned cash. How dare someone violate the sanctity of one's web history—it's cruel, I tell you!

He was about to give me his phone when his eyes widened at the smirk on my face as I gripped the bat. The house wasn't as large and lavish as it looked on the video feed, not nearly big enough to produce an echo, but if anyone else was home, sitting in the furthest corner of the farthest room, they most certainly heard the vibrating ring of aluminum.

***

Donald finally woke up and immediately, as I predicted, he started tugging on his wrist and ankle restraints. I didn't say anything.

He'll tucker himself out like a toddler with a new shiny toy, I thought.

I sat on a small stool, admiring his spacious garage. It was odd to see, however, that a man like himself wouldn't have a set of tools anywhere around here. Just floral-patterned patio furniture and stowaway garden gnomes. A lot of sewing material, too.

He gave up trying to break free after ten minutes (I thought the sonofabitch would put up a fight for at least an hour). His conquered body slid back in his chair like spineless jelly.

"I changed my email password," I told him, fiddling with my baseball bat. "So I should never hear from you again, right?"

Muffled words came out so I peeled back the duct tape over his mouth. He let out a painful yelp.

"I'm so sorry, sir, *please*—"

I put a finger over my lips. "Shhhh. You have to be quieter."

He started weeping, then he spoke softly. "I'm sorry, sir. *So* sorry. Please, whatever you paid me I'll give it back, just please let me go."

"How can I let you go after all the damage you've done? I mean, look at this place. Clearly, you've made quite a fortune from scamming all these vulnerable people."

"No sir, please, you have to understand—this isn't my place. This is my grandmother's. She's very sick. She needs medicine! It's very expensive—"

"Yeah, yeah, sure. Sounds likely. Now, where are you storing my web history?"

Donald looked at me like he'd seen a ghost. "I—I don't know what you mean."

"Let me say it again, nicely." I gripped the bat and drove it into his thigh. This time he started wailing so I put the duct tape back over his mouth. "Where are you storing my web history? I need you to tell me so I can find it."

Tears came out of the corners of his eyes and he started mumbling again. He already knew what I'd looked at. Such disgusting acts—one might willingly blind themselves if they saw it for themselves. Donald must not have seen it for himself. His eyes still worked quite well. He must have only seen the raw data. I told him I'd take the duct tape off if he promised not to scream. He nodded and I released his lips.

"Please, you have to believe me. I don't know your history. Please, please let me go and I won't say anything."

And I wanted to believe him, but you can never trust a criminal. Even if they show up at your door with a dead car battery and a faulty cell phone. I put the duct tape back over his mouth and swung the bat at his restrained hand. He squirmed in pain, muffling a slew of phrases and what I assumed were expletives. He tried releasing his other hand from its restraint to caress the other but he couldn't break free. His tears really started to flow.

I'll give him one more chance, I decided. I was feeling quite chipper today.

I peeled off the duct tape and bent down so that our eyes were level. I stared into his frightened eyes with military-grade focus, and calmly asked him for the location of my stored web history, but sadly his answer didn't change nor did my decision to grip the aluminum bat and cock it back behind my shoulder, but before I could swing at his fragile skull, the side door creaked open and a pair of small plastic shoes clacked on the floor.

She stood there at the entrance, gawking at me like she had forgotten to add sugar to my coffee. Her stance was that of a frightened doe, and if I wasn't mere seconds away from swinging, I might have said something nice to her. But I didn't say anything. I just gave her the same revolted look she was familiar with.

Her lips quivered as they tried to let the words out. That little molasses-brown mole that sat right above her right lip jiggled with all that quivering. How I do love that mole of hers, as if God made a perfect girl for me but then snuck in a reminder that nobody, not even my perfect Dolly, was without flaws. Her lips finally parted.

"Make sure you choke up on your grip," she nervously said, scratching her arm at some invisible rash. "Or else your wrists will hurt after."

I smiled at her. She gave a curled smile back and ushered herself back to the car. A lovely Dolly she was when she listened. If only my incompetent nymphet could follow directions to make a good cup of coffee.

I looked back at Donald who was giving me sorrowful eyes and for a second, I felt a bit of envy for the poor bastard. Some people are evil and others are just trying to survive. A crook, yes, but also a flawed machine that needs to be repaired. He's fortunate, like all the other salvageable people in this world. He's lucky he's in this place, I concluded, for I am a broken machine that cannot be fixed.

I took Dolly's advice, choked up my grip on the bat, and swung it with intense force—which was closely followed by extensive cleaning of the garage.

When I went back outside after a good amount of time, Dolly was sitting on the sidewalk next to our parked car, playing with stones.

"I was a good girl back there, wasn't I?" she said, compelling me to agree with her.

I gave an unenthusiastic nod.

"Where are we going?" she asked.

"It's a surprise, my love."

"I don't like surprises."

"You'll like this one."

"Is it a *puppy*? Are we getting a puppy?"

"No, we're not."

"Why not? I've been such a good girl. I want a puppy. You promised me a puppy!"

I grabbed her arm and tugged her toward me.

"There will be *no* speaking of this puppy business from now on, do you understand?"

I held her hard by her knobby wrist with a vice grip strong enough to make it snap if she thrashed with enough force. I could see her holding back tears as we walked. She knew not to let her emotions out. A good girl she was—at least she was right about that. I wanted her to sit next to me at the front of the car so I could caress her exposed thigh, but I also had to punish her.

I threw her into the backseat of the car among the empty grocery bags and scattered clothes. She cried something incomprehensible. With a mighty roar, we peeled out of the neighborhood, painting the asphalt with tire tracks

and almost hitting a troublesome suburban dog as we
ferociously drove away.

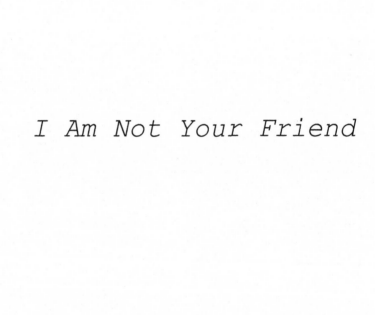

I Am Not Your Friend

A giant billboard in a frame of lightbulbs stood on Highway 27. A new exhibit at Stenson Candi's World Famous Circus had just opened up.

Entertaining. Engaging. Wowing.

Those were some of the adjectives written on the billboard.

I had passed by the circus many times while taking the 27, but I never stopped in. Mainly because I had been so busy. I was on my way to see Mom, who had become very ill, and I didn't have many friends so I devoted all my love and care and attention to her and only her. On my way back from the nursing home, I decided to stop by the circus to see what sort of exhibit could demand such a spectacular sign on a popular highway.

I was wedged between two burly men in a sea of spectators, all of us looking at the entertaining, engaging, wowing, exhibit. One would think an exhibit with those associated adjectives would host a fire eater or an exotic creature or a bearded man with twelve fingers, but, as I stood up on my tippy toes to see above the crowd of hairy heads, I only saw one person sitting at a table.

He was a teenager, thin and attractive, with wispy blonde hair. A wooden sign was painted gaily and hung above his exhibit. It read PERCY THE ENTERTAINER. Sitting in his exhibit—a sort of nice cage with cushions, a table, a mattress, a sink, and a bathroom shrouded by a curtain—was Percy.

On the table in front of him was a stack of at least a hundred pieces of paper.

"Make a paper airplane!" one of the spectators shouted.

"You should do more painting like you did last week," another shouted.

"What are you making?" yelled a third.

"I'm trying to make a crane," Percy finally said to the crowd, fidgeting the paper with his fingers. "Revolting origami, what tortured soul came up with this?"

Percy made an incorrect fold with the paper and slammed his hands on the table. He crumbled the piece of paper and threw it over his shoulder.

"I believe any sane man would put a bullet in his head before deciding to play with paper for fun," he exclaimed.

The crowd started laughing. The two burly men beside me were holding their stomachs. I had never seen someone half my age speak so well and so humorously.

"You need to keep your hands steady!" someone from the crowd shouted.

"Try making a tulip flower. Those are a pain in the ass," another shouted.

"My hands *are* goddamn steady!" Percy shouted to the crowd as he fiddled with the paper, folding it with care until he eventually made another tear. "I'm starting to think the sword swallowers have it easier."

Laughter erupted from the crowd. Percy tried to make three paper cranes, which eventually took two hours, and in none of that time did the crowd shrink. If anything, it got bigger. And in all that time, he was cracking jokes.

"That's your girlfriend?" he called out to a couple near the front of the crowd. The man was overweight, balding, and had bad posture. His girlfriend was slim and toned with vivacious red hair. "There's just no way. You must be paying her a pretty penny," he joked at him. "I had a girlfriend a while back, but she left me for a juggler. I guess she wanted someone who was good with his hands. Now you see why I'm doing origami." The couple laughed. So did the crowd. And they always felt the urge to try to talk to Percy, hoping he would respond.

"She sounds like a bore!" someone shouted.

"You should ask out the bearded lady in the other exhibit," another yelled.

I even felt an urge to say something to him.

"Maybe you'll find better luck with a carney matchmaker," I yelled, somehow restraining my chuckle.

"I'm not going on any dates until I master the ancient art of origami," Percy said without diverting his eyes away from his hands, folding a fresh piece of paper. "I can't go on any dates right now. What would I say? *'Hey I'm Percy. I live in a cage and play with paper.'* "

Percy kept us enthralled with jokes. He also told stories about his past, working as a street performer, which were often interrupted by brief stings of rage when he tore the paper or folded it incorrectly. When Percy finally finished the third crane, the crowd thundered with applause.

"Thank you, thank you," he sarcastically said. "This is applause suitable for a Nobel prize winner." He looked over at the two other cranes sitting on the desk in front of him, then down at the third one he just made in his hands. "Well, I already have two of these damn things. No need to have three. Hey, you!"

He pointed out his finger, and although to me it looked like a blurry digit since I was so far from the exhibit, so congested with the others in the crowd, it was pointing directly at me. I was taken off guard.

"Me?" I cowardly asked.

"Yeah you, superstar. Here, pass this crane over to that lucky guy. He looks like he's had a hard day today."

From the front of the crowd, the crane was delicately passed back between people until it reached my hands—and that's when I was put under Percy's spell.

He exuded confidence, and was so sure of himself at his young age. Percy wasn't old enough to buy cigarettes but was able to entertain a crowd of hundreds of people. His sharp and shrewd commentary, his chaotic sense of humor, his relatability. It wasn't like watching the sword swallower or the juggler, and while sticking a sword down your throat all the way to the hilt and juggling ten random objects in the air are impressive acts, they can be done by anybody with the necessary skills. Percy, however, could do the most mundane and make it the most extraordinary. Everyone in the crowd wanted to be his friend—and when I held that paper crane in my hand, I wanted to be his friend.

The impresario came out in front of the exhibit and announced that it was time for a dance break. Loud dance music blared from speakers inside the exhibit and Percy jumped to his feet and started dancing.

"I always use contraceptives but my doctor told me that my dancing would be just as effective." He started shaking his hips and throwing his hands in the air. "No way a baby would want to be born to a father who dances like this."

A burst of laughter came from the crowd, and while Percy's self-deprecation was humorous, it was the furthest from accurate. He contorted his body in a way that was more fluid than a river of water squishing past rocks and weaving itself through forests and hills and mountains. He was a gifted dancer, and when Percy was done dancing, a thunderous applause came from the crowd. I felt myself clapping too, and I rarely clapped at anything.

—

"So then Percy starts with a fresh sheet of paper, right? But only five minutes into it, he already rips it!" I laughed to myself. Mom laid on her lumpy bed and just smiled. "So he crumbles the ripped paper and tosses it to a woman in the crowd and tells her 'Lucky you. You get a free souvenir'. "

Mom again, just smiled. Her room in the nursing home was beige. A very boring beige. There was a wooden nightstand next to her bed with a stack of magazines and a bundle of fake sunflowers that sat in a blue vase. The room was made to be safe, since the outside world was too harsh for Mom. At least the upholstered rocking chair I was sitting in was comfortable.

"And after he finishes the three paper cranes, he tells the crowd to hand one of them to me. He gave it to *me*, of all people! Can you believe that?"

"That's very nice, dear," she finally said in a croaky voice. "It's very nice to see you. It's been tough these past few days."

"You know, me and Percy could work together as street performers. I would do some sort of juggling act that I could learn over time, and really, it would be less about the juggling and more about my personality that would draw people in, and Percy would just be Percy. And people would love us!"

The nurse came in with a tray of tomato soup, a glass of water, and a small paper cup of different colored pills.

"Thank you," Mom said to the nurse, who smiled and left. She picked up the plastic spoon with a veiny hand. It was shaking uncontrollably.

"Do you think I could be a good juggler?" I asked Mom. "Obviously it won't be about my juggling and more about me, but I have to be somewhat good, you know?"

Her veiny hand was shaking with a spoonful of tomato soup, which she delicately brought to her withered lips.

"I think I'd be really good. I wonder how long it would take to learn it? Percy can help me learn. He's a carney, so he must know something."

Mom's hand shook so much that barely a drop of tomato soup was left on the spoon when it reached her mouth. Trying to bring the spoon back down, her shaking hand accidentally dropped it in the bowl of tomato soup.

"Oh, dear," she said.

"I could also just make paper cranes. Percy already knows how to do that, and he can teach me. But I do think I can juggle. Maybe if I start with something small."

While mom was trying to fish the spoon out of her bowl of tomato soup, I took the colorful pills out of the small paper cup and started juggling them.

"Maybe this is how I'll start," I said.

I got two of them in the air, and caught both. Then I threw three of them in the air and dropped all of them on the floor. Mom looked over at me, then pressed a button on the remote to call the nurse in.

—

The nursing home said visiting hours were cut off after three in the afternoon, but I had to see Percy again. I saw the glaring billboard in the lightbulb frame and took a hard right off Highway 27. I phoned the nursing home and pleaded for them to make an exception.

"I'm sorry, sir. After three, we don't allow visits."

Absolute, arbitrary bullshit. I scorned the woman on the other end of the phone and hung up.

This time I was squeezed between another teenager and an older woman. The crowd had doubled in size, with all their attention on Percy who was playing the harmonica while telling stories about his time working as a stagehand for a traveling circus.

"One of the knives slipped out of the juggler's fingers and I almost got beheaded," he said in a deadpan tone. "That was almost an opportunity for me to file a lawsuit and live off the settlement, but unfortunately, as you can see—" and Percy started stretching his neck to each side "—my head's still attached, so I'm stuck here playing this stupid toy for all of you."

He blew into the harmonica and a sad wail came out of it. The audience erupted with laughter. People started shouting things to Percy.

"Stuck playing the harmonica for us!"

"Do you know anything by the Windchime Band?"

"What's your favorite type of drink?"

"Sprite," Percy said to the crowd. "A cold can of Sprite. If I could, I'd only drink Sprite."

I'd never had Sprite, but I loved Pepsi. It was the thing Mom always brought in a cooler on summer beach days. He's too young to have rum, but I imagined me and Percy could get along over a can of Sprite.

He told more stories about his past, talked about his favorite movies and music and hobbies on a sunny afternoon.

He spoke about himself for a long time, long enough for a bitter spectator to heckle from the crowd. "Galileo called, the world doesn't revolve around you."

Percy replied, "It actually does revolve around me, and you're lucky to be in my orbit."

The crowd erupted with laughter. So did the heckler.

I stayed there for a few more hours, watching Percy tell more stories while trying to learn the beginning of a Windchime Band song on the harmonica until I got a phone call from the nursing home.

—

Percy had looked a bit weaker today than usual.

I may have missed something in the past few days. I had to work, and when I wasn't working, I was with Mom. She was getting worse. Her illness was ravaging her.

Percy's neck was slimmer and his figure was more lean and slender. Maybe he was just always like that. Percy tended to wear baggy clothes that draped over his body, but he looked noticeably weaker, deader in the eyes, like a needle was injected into his flimsy arm and sucked out his energy. Nonetheless, there was an enormous crowd surrounding him.

A wooden sign hung next to his exhibit.

THREE DAYS OF LIVING OFF ONLY CELERY.

Percy just sat there on the couch in his exhibit, lying on his back with his hands behind his neck. He wasn't doing anything, but the crowd was just as large and just as awestruck at observing him.

"Don't worry, everybody," Percy said to the audience. "Celery contains a massive amount of nutrition. Like the fifteen calories I get from eating two of these giant celery stalks." He then held up one of the stalks, which was almost the size of a baseball bat. "Never mind all my vitamin and nutrient deficiencies," he said, then took a large, crunchy bite.

The fast went on for a few more days, and I visited Percy every day of it. People wanted to see Percy succeed so they walked up to his exhibit to give him gifts. A woman had brought him a Rubik's Cube, telling him it was good to engage in some activity to keep his mind off the hunger. Everyone marveled as he played around with it. Another person brought a plush blanket. It didn't help with the fasting, but I assumed the man felt that Percy was cold.

Another brought some hunger-inhibiting tea, which he drank non-stop. I brought him a rubber mat so he could practice meditation or do some yoga.

"I'm probably the least enlightened person in a five-hundred-mile radius, but I'll try. Thanks," Percy said to me, folding up the mat and putting it by his bed.

Percy spent the next few hours telling entertaining personal stories and playing with the Rubik's Cube to distract himself from his stomach. The crowd was getting more congested. I bumped shoulders with everyone around me. People were shoving themselves forward, trying to get closer to Percy.

"Try and solve it as fast as you can," someone from the crowd shouted.

Someone's elbow accidentally dug into my back from behind.

"Celery is awful, I'd never eat it!" yelled another.

"You should do yoga on the rubber mat instead!" I shouted to him, but he didn't hear me.

—

"Will you need any bags?" the grocery clerk asked.

"No thanks," I told her.

She nodded, waited for the four cases of Sprite to come down the conveyor belt, and scanned their barcodes.

"That's a lot of Sprite," the clerk said.

"Yeah, it's for me and my friend."

"You're gonna drink all of this?"

"More so my friend. Sprite's his favorite."

"I can see that."

The machine burped out a receipt and the clerk handed it to me. I thanked her and went back to my car. I opened one of the cans and took a sip and by God, it was one of the best things I'd ever tasted. Dare I say, better than Pepsi.

—

After Mom died, I went to see Percy more often. I couldn't see him yesterday because I had to handle all of Mom's affairs, and I wouldn't be able to see him this coming Saturday because of the funeral, but I was able to see him today.

I tried to get to his exhibit as early as possible. He started at nine in the morning so I got there at seven, waiting outside the entrance with my four cases of Sprite. About a dozen or so others were waiting with me. Waiting for Percy. A kid had brought a case of Sprite and was sitting on it while throwing rocks at a wooden pole.

Only one case? I brought four, you dope.

Finally, the doors opened.

Before reaching Percy's exhibit, there were a few other exhibits that I hadn't really noticed before. A sword-swallower, a juggler (who I hope wasn't the same one that Percy's old partner left him for), a woman in laced clothing dancing to a pop song, a young boy covering himself in grape jelly, and a bearded lady. All the exhibits had small crowds gathered around them, but none like Percy's.

Because I was so early, I got a spot close to the front of his exhibit, dragging my cases of Sprite with me. I was eventually smushed by the incoming crowd of people coming to see him. The large black blanket that covered his exhibit was pulled off, and Percy was sitting on his couch, chomping on a piece of celery.

"I don't need to do this anymore," he sardonically said to the crowd. He then pointed to the wooden sign.

SEVEN DAYS OF LIVING OFF ONLY CELERY.

"That's as many days as I could've gone," he said. "And I could have gone longer if the impresario didn't cut me off due to medical risks." He emphasized "medical risks" with mocking air quotes.

The crowd started booing, showing their disdain for the impresario, who was somewhere nobody knew.

"You could have gone at least two weeks," someone from the crowd shouted.

"Maybe another few days!" another shouted.

"Do another fast but with orange juice," a third yelled.

Percy rolled his eyes and exhaled dramatically. He didn't respond to any of them. He flailed his arm up without care, flaccidly alerting someone.

"Might as well get the new sign up," he said in a deflated tone.

A carney worker came from behind the exhibit to remove the wooden sign. He replaced it with a new one.

SAMPLING THE BEST OF MEATS.

A plate of exquisite meats was brought inside of his exhibit and placed on the table. He got up from the couch to go sit at the table. His movements were sluggish and lumbering, like an animal who had just come out of a deep sleep. He slumped down in the chair in front of the table, looking down at the assortment of meats, each spread with different toppings. He lazily licked his lips, and didn't say anything for a bit. Then he started eating.

The man who was once on track to skeleton-thinness was now gorging himself like a voracious panther. With each bite, he munched and chewed, sometimes making tasteful humming noises or simply spitting the meat onto the floor. There wasn't much commentary or witty banter or enthralling stories from his past. There was just eating.

I shouted at him, offering a can of Sprite, but he didn't respond. He just kept eating. At one point, Percy discarded a chewed-up piece of a buffalo chicken burger to the floor.

—

Later that night, I dreamed of me and Percy performing a street show, me juggling with masterful balance and Percy just being Percy. And after we made our money, thousands of dollars of donations and tickets, I'd take him to Scooter's so he could sink his teeth into a burger he wouldn't spit onto the floor and curse at. Once he took a bite into one of Scooter's deluxe chicken burgers, his eyes would light up like the bulbs on his billboard. "This is so good, I wouldn't even share this with my dog," I'd say to him while taking a bite, and he'd smile back.

—

"Does anybody have a song request for me to dance to?" Percy sluggishly said to the crowd.

A shout came from the back.

"Harmonica! Let's see you play it!"

A roar of cheers followed and Percy rolled his eyes and slumped his shoulders.

"I mean sure, it's your decision. But I'm not any better than I was a few days ago."

He took the harmonica out of its case and started playing a few riffs. The audience loved it, and so did I. Percy was naturally talented. The crowd felt a bit smaller than before. I had space to flare out my elbows, but Percy still attracted a crowd of enamored spectators.

Halfway through, he lost wind and stopped playing.

"I wish I knew guitar," he moaned. "That's a *real* instrument."

"My brother's really good at guitar, he can teach you!" someone from the crowd shouted.

"Better to know piano," another yelled.

Percy ignored them. He pulled out a piece of paper from a drawer and slumped onto the couch, trying to fold the paper into an elegant crane until he tore the side of it, and he yelled a revolting slew of words at it that made the veins in his neck pop out and his face turn red with contaminated rage. It was a disgusting tirade of anger and bitter hostility. It was naive and childish of him. He crumpled the crane and threw it out into the crowd.

"Stupid piece of shit," he yelled.

The person who caught the crumpled crane held it for a moment before dropping it to the ground like a foul-smelling piece of trash, and I could instinctively feel a collective agreement from the crowd that they would have all done the same.

—

It was okay for Percy to cancel a show on all of us at the last minute, but after the fourth time, it became a nuisance. The crowd stood there with furrowed eyebrows and buried hands in pockets.

"I'm sorry!" the impresario addressed the crowd, standing in front of Percy's exhibit, which was draped with that large black blanket. "He's mighty sick today and won't be able to perform."

The crowd collectively groaned.

"Good people! We have plenty of other exhibits that I promise will satisfy your thirst for entertainment!"

The crowd was skeptical, and then scattered about to the other exhibits.

I decided to go home and get some rest before the funeral tomorrow.

———

Over time, Percy's crowd slowly dwindled in number, and it was only a few weeks later when I showed up to his exhibit and the place was nearly deserted.

Percy had put less effort in his acts. He seemed burnt out. Uninspired to do anything, and the people in the crowd grew less and less entertained as the days went by.

One day, Percy was trying to build a table, but did so in a way where it felt more like a chore than an enjoyable activity. He mumbled the instructions to himself and proceeded to follow them. He didn't make any jokes or tell any humorous stories from his past. It felt as if all of us were looking into someone's home from a windowpane, uninvited and unentertained.

On another day, Percy was sampling different kinds of cheese, and he would eat a piece of cheese and simply say "that was good" or "that wasn't good" and nothing else.

Even the impresario noticed Percy's lackluster effort, so occasionally, he would have Percy do dance breaks. Percy wouldn't dance. Instead, he'd jerk his arms around and sway from side to side, like a depressed palm tree, nudged by a determined wind.

One day I think Percy reached his breaking point.

He laid in bed all day, not uttering a single word to the crowd during his six hour show.

"Are you okay?" one of the spectators asked.

"You should dance to a Regina Styles song," another said.

He didn't respond to either of them, or to anyone that day. He laid in bed like an inert block of wood. He had no interest in putting on a show. He occasionally mumbled something to himself in anger, but I couldn't decipher what he was saying.

No show meant no entertainment, so the crowds shrank each day. Percy became more agitated toward life itself as his loyal crowd of spectators started to diminish.

His billboard was changed to advertise a new entertainer, someone more amusing, vivacious, and entertaining than Percy. To get to the new exhibit, attendees had to pass by Percy's, which was barren and without any interest. Some of them made swift eye contact with me before darting their eyes away and picking up their feet to get a good place in the crowd at the new exhibit. Percy was lying on his back on the couch in his exhibit when I went to see him. His neck was even thinner than before and his arms were spindly like scissor blades.

"Seven *dreadful* days," he said to nobody in particular. "That's child's play. I can go longer. The people will come and see."

He took a huge bite from a celery stick held in his hand. A new but similar wooden sign hung next to his exhibit.

THREE DAYS OF EATING ONLY CELERY, AND COUNTING.

Percy looked disheartened, like he had failed to become what he had wanted to be all his life. I went up to his exhibit and knocked on the bars.

"No petting," he growled.

"Yeah, you need to get a sign," I said to him.

His gaze passed over me, like there was a huge crowd of people in front of him that he was addressing. "When people pet me," he said to nobody in particular. "I get a little stabby-stabby." He pantomimed a swift stabbing motion with his hand while still lying on the couch.

I assumed he would seek some sort of refuge or shelter from the embarrassment in his exhibit by staying in bed or shrouded in the bathroom, but he just sat on his couch. I felt bad for Percy, that this loss of interest from the public could bring on an intense feeling of regret and melancholy. I wanted to be there for him. To help him weather the storm.

"Hey, you know what would be great?" I said to him softly. "There's this buffalo chicken burger place in my hometown that I think you'd love. You just gotta give it a chance. I bet you'll have a change of heart with just one bite. And after that, we can—"

"Okay. Look, man," he said, turning his head to face me, finally addressing me. "Get this straight in your head—I am not your friend. I am a body of entertainment. If I'm not entertaining you, stop watching me." He turned his head back to look at the ceiling and took another bite of celery. "I think the most psychopathic person in the world is someone who eats celery and makes paper cranes," he said to nobody in particular. He let out a few nasty coughs.

Deflated and disappointed, I walked over to the other exhibit, which was filled with enamored spectators like the ones that used to crowd around Percy. I stood among the crowd of spectators. The exhibit was a young woman, around Percy's age, playing trivia while wearing a shock collar. She didn't know the United States owned Puerto Rico so she was electrocuted at the neck and let out a painful wail. She started laughing at her stupidity and the crowd joined in as well.

"In fairness, I probably wouldn't have gotten that question either," one of the spectators said to me.

"Same here, I only know the Virgin Islands because that's how people in high school referred to the improv and band club." The spectator smiled at me. He was an older man with gray stubble and a vulpine jaw. He was holding the hand of his daughter. Her expression was blank and she was wearing a yellow shirt of patterned daisies. She didn't say a word, but me and the older man did. As the day went on, we chatted over the sound of painful wails and thunderous applause.

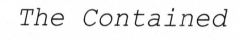

The Contained

I wanted today to be different, so I left my micro-dwelling to pick up a bundle of bananas at the little market on the other side of the city. Today was going to be different.

Yesterday was a typical day of digital labor, making sure micro-transactions were accurate and confirming them on my floatscreen. Most work was done on the floatscreen, and everything else that couldn't be handled on there was shipped directly to their homes. Their micro-dwellings.

After my dedicated labor hours, I played Star Slashers on my companion, which was a little floatscreen I could put in my pocket. Then I felt a throbbing in my crotch and knew I was overdue for a release, which didn't take more than a few minutes with the help of the release-aids you can find online. The release was mechanical and chore-like. And the throbbing went away just as Dr. Rhinehart said it would. After my release, I took a shower and moisturized my body, mostly my crotch area because it felt sore.

Then I watched snippets for a few more hours on my floatscreen. They were no longer than a few seconds so I didn't feel bored, and they usually played right after the other. Sometimes when I got up to get food from my kitchen,

I would have to replay a snippet because I would miss the whole thing! The company that hosted the snippets had this great tagline. A woman with a soothing voice like Momma would say, "With so many different snippets, there's always something to watch!"

It was true.

There was always something to watch.

And thank goodness there was because there were times when I would sit in my micro-dwelling and hear the slightest creak of wood or the smallest bug scuttle on the floor, and I would feel not happy. Not *sti-mule-ated*.

I haven't heard that word in a long time. Dr. Rhinehart used that word once. He said that *sti-mule-ated* means interested, a sort of happy feeling. That's why we have the floatscreens and the companions and the mega-markets and the release-aids and the snippets. For the happy feeling.

I remembered one day while I was waiting for one of the auto-mechanics to come repair my floatscreen, I decided to look out the small window in the corner of my micro-dwelling. I couldn't see much out of it since it was very small. I could only see the other walls of my complex where other people lived in their micro-dwellings. Most of them kept a shade over their windows but one of them was open. I squished my eyes real tight and saw a man with no hair slumped over his couch with both hands covering his eyes like he was playing hide and go seek. His room was very dark, just like mine, and the glare of his floatscreen reflected onto his chest.

I didn't like to feel this way.

And I felt that I wasn't the only person who felt this way, but I didn't know for sure if others felt the same way because people didn't talk to each other no more. But I would think that they did. I'd think this way when I would sit in my micro-dwelling and it'd be very cold and very quiet. That's when I'd watch my snippets or play my game because it got a little warmer and a little less quiet.

Momma used to make things loud and warm. She used to mummy-wrap me in blankets when I was cold and make rice pudding and sing when it was quiet. And when I was too scared to sleep, she would open all the doors of my closet, poke her head in and say, "Nope. No monsters in here."

She's not around no more—that is, until yesterday when I got a piece of her back.

The automated estate process gave me her old record player. It was the only thing she had left in my name. She also left me her records, but each time I put one on the player, it was still very cold and very quiet, so I threw them all down the waste chute. I looked at the player until I couldn't look at it no more. I decided it was better to go out and buy bananas.

~

"The medication isn't working," Dr. Rhinehart sternly told my mother.

I was sitting in the corner of the room playing with some of the toys in his office. They put earphones on me that played soothing music, but you could stop the music by pressing a little button on the side of it. They didn't know I had found this button.

They think our brains are mush by this age. And they're right to think that, which is why they also think I'm actually taking the medication. How easy it is to put a pill in your mouth when your mother is watching and then spit it back in your hand and hide it when she turns away.

"I don't understand," my worried mother said to him. "What can we do? He's already twelve and his behavior isn't getting any better."

I didn't look over to see her face but she sounded distraught. I kept playing with my theraspheres, rolling them on the white stoned, antiseptic floor. If you don't bounce them on the ground and release the chemicals inside, like most kids do, then they don't lull your brain to paralysis. To Dr. Rhinehart and my mother, I looked innocuous.

"I's difficult," Dr. Rhinehart said. "His mind is clearly poisoned. But when he starts to poison others is when we have a real problem."

"What do you mean?"

"His words are influencing others. And it's creating a harmful environment."

"Oh, dear."

I glanced over at my mother. She was clutching her companion in her hands. What is a mother to do? I told her about the book. Told her many times, but she never listened. She listened to Dr. Rhinehart, to the other mothers, to the patrollers, even the corrupt, awful council.

"His mind is poisoned?" she asked.

"Very much so," Dr. Rhinehart assured her.

"But he acts so rebellious."

"I would too if I believed this place was a prison. I don't have bars over my windows. I'm not wearing an orange jumpsuit. This place is anything but a prison. If anything, the prison is outside of here. You can go to the lookout point and see for yourself. It's a wasteland. There's nothing left."

My ears twitched when he said that.

The lookout point?

"I don't want to go to that horrible place," my mother said. "I've heard enough about it to stay away from there."

"Well, it's quite difficult from here. I'm hesitant to report him, since they'd have to shock him." Dr. Rhinehart then clasped his hands and rested them on the large brown desk in front of him. "And I know that could be very hard for a mother to deal with."

My mother took a soft, microfiber cloth from her bag and wiped her hands with it. Dr. Rhinehart nodded. Then said: "But if he keeps up this kind of behavior, I may not have a choice."

And then I thought, you always have a choice.

~

The little market was too far to walk to so I headed to the underground subway station. The streets were quiet, as they usually were. They were very clean and the buildings stood high in the sky. Many people lived here but rarely did they leave their micro-dwellings. A few machines hummed as they unloaded large waste bins and a flock of pigeons was bathing in one of the marble fountains. One of them lost its footing and slipped. It started twitching, and little blue sparks flew out of its body until the water completely covered it.

I walked past a mega-market.

Its wide presence took up the entire block and its clear walls let you peek inside.

When I was smaller, Momma would take me to the little market near our home. We only went inside a few times since it was easier to talk to the machine out front, but inside, they had different kinds of fruits and vegetables and cultured meats. There was also a small baked goods section where Momma used to buy me a sugar cookie if I had finished my schoolwork that evening.

When the new mega-markets started to open everywhere, Momma would take me there all the time. It was more convenient and they had more selection, she told me. She took me there until I was old enough to go myself, and I couldn't believe the selection they had. Almost every type of food you could think of, already made. They even delivered nutritious meals and ingredients right to your micro-dwelling!

A man in tattered clothing with a bright red nose was sitting outside of the mega-market, eating from a plastic container of gocaberries until he threw up a jet of red sludge onto the sidewalk. He then wiped his mouth and continued to eat from the container. I couldn't tell whether they popped or smushed.

I stopped thinking about gocaberries and headed for the subway station.

~

"I like your blouse."

The woman didn't respond, unmoved by my words. She kept looking at her companion. I knew I said them. I knew she heard me.

"I think I need to try again," I whispered to my little sister, sitting next to me with swollen eyes. Our mother was distracted with her companion, watching snippets about baking recipes.

There was a tense silence in the subway car. One of the rules on the passenger conduct sign was to **respect the privacy of others**.

"Excuse me," I said a bit louder. This time the woman shivered like a wet dog and looked up from her companion. *"I like your blouse,"* I said to her, but the woman stared at me with widened eyes for a few seconds before looking back down at her companion.

I grunted, then turned to my little sister. *"Why does everyone walk around with pursed lips? And when you speak to them, why are they always so startled?"*

Our mother looked up from her companion. *"What are you doing?"*

I glanced over at a man, who made eye contact with me for a brief moment before darting his eyes away to continue eating. *"And why when you look at people, do they look away as if I was some hideous creature?"*

"Please stop that," she scolded me.

"Why is nobody listening to me? It's as if I'm speaking nonsense. I'm not! Not in the slightest! You've all let your minds be pounded to mush."

A few passengers' eyes looked up at me, then retreated back to their companions. One woman who was asleep with an earbud in, let out a croaky, painful sound, and twisted to her other side, revealing a puffy, swollen ear.

I was furious. I walked up to the woman in the nice blouse and slapped the companion out of her hands. "Keep your eyes off that disgusting thing! There's a whole world around you. And you're trapped inside this prison!"

Our mother lunged at me, constricting me with her arms. I kept yelling until the subway car screeched to a halt. The doors opened and four patrollers came onboard and dragged me out. Up the stairs and back onto the street, they loaded me into a vehicle that was to transport me to the place where they zap your brain, but before they could put me in it, I tilted my neck as far back as it went and looked up. A blanket of artificial dots speckled the faultless ceiling. And I knew that it would be the last time I'd see the ceiling and it would soon be the first time I saw the sky like everybody else.

Sam Calvo

~

The subway approached the waiting platform, hissing to a halt, and opened its sliding doors. I took my seat and played a game on my companion.

My favorite game was Star Slashers. Boy, it used to be fun. You played as this little spaceship and you had to blast all these incoming rocks before they hit you. I remembered feeling so good after each level, but now I played games to pass the time. When I completed a level, I read on the screen that I had won the level and I simply understood that I was going to the next level of the game. After beating the last level, a gilded banner popped up on the screen saying "Congratulations! Want to play again?" I would read the banner and understand that there was no more game for me to play unless I wanted to start over. I usually restarted the game but sometimes I would play Gold Seekers or Ninja Attack or Tank Invaders if I wanted to.

Today, I was playing Star Slashers on the subway. Another person was playing Tank Invaders and another was eating from a pint of ice cream.

The woman sitting next to me was playing Dragon Hunters, which was a game I had not played before but I heard that it got expensive because there were things in the game you could buy. It was popular among kids because it was the most entertaining. I remembered I was in the subway car and this mother was with her baby daughter who started crying. And the baby cried and cried. The mother looked exhausted. She was carrying six bags of groceries from the mega-market and looked like she didn't know what to do. How difficult it must be to stop the crying of a person you can't talk to! But then she gave her baby daughter her companion to play Dragon Hunters and the crying stopped, and the mother was relieved, and all of us on the subway car were relieved.

Fortunately today, there was no crying baby.

Then the doors of the subway car opened to nobody.

I got off the subway and walked up the stairs to the streets. I passed by a group of kids sitting on the marble steps of an old government building. It was still so cold, so I buried my chin into the neck of my shirt and walked toward the little market.

~

"Say hi to the nice screen, Mordy!"

We were standing outside the little market, and Momma was pointing to the screen which sat inside the face of a friendly machine. I knew the word hi, but it was difficult to say. It had already been four days since the procedure but I was still unable to speak. The screen showed two digital eyes and a digital smiling mouth. My mouth struggled to form the words.

"Can you wave to the nice machine?" Momma asked, and I was able to lift my arm up and do a sort of crooked wave with a limp wrist. A friendly waving hand appeared on screen.

"Very good!" she congratulated me. "I'm so proud of you." She then looked at the machine. "We'll take three bundles of bananas, a carton of nutrient liquid, five packages of chocolate cubes, a six pound bag of flavoring paste," then she looked at me and smiled, "and thirteen candles for a special someone's birthday."

All the things Momma asked for appeared on the screen. Then a digital happy face appeared and asked if she needed anything else.

I was thirsty, but I couldn't speak. It felt so difficult. My tongue had been tangled or my mind had been scrambled. I wanted to cry. I was thirsty but I couldn't say it.

I just kept pointing to the entrance of the little market that stood next to the friendly robot. I'm thirsty! I'm thirsty! I wanted to say, but I couldn't. My eyes started to water and I felt the liquid coming out of them. Then I felt Momma's loving hands wrap around me.

"It's okay, baby. It's okay." She gently caressed my back. "Dr. Rhinehart says the first few days after the procedure are tough. But you'll be back to yourself soon. I promise you, love."

She kissed my head, then told the machine that we had everything we wanted. Seconds later, all the items were wrapped in a bag and came out of a small opening and onto a counter near the large door. She grabbed the items, then my delicate hand, and we walked back home.

I kept crying.

~

The machine in front of the little market was gone, and the large door that was usually closed off was open. Inside were shelves and displays of all the packaged food. I walked through the large door and saw a young woman sitting behind a counter, scribbling something onto a piece of paper. She was the only person in the market, besides the machines that worked in the back. Most places were run by the machines so it was very odd that she worked there. She looked up at me.

"Hello," she said.

I looked back at the entrance of the market and then back to her. "The machine out front is gone," I said to her.

"Rest of the place will be gone soon."

"Oh."

There was a brief silence.

"Machines still work in the back," she informed me.

"That's good."

"The mega-market has all our stuff and more."

"Yes, it does."

She nodded.

"Traffic's still bad too."

"Mmh."

She scribbled something onto the same piece of paper. Her handwriting was difficult to read, unlike the letters on my floatscreen and my companion, which were always clear.

"I used to come here with my Momma as a kid," I told her.

"I see."

"Do you have bananas?"

"We do."

She walked around the counter and guided me to the back of the market where bundles of bright yellow bananas sat in a suspended basket.

"Bananas have potassium," she said. "The potassium is good for the body."

It was good to hear that since Dr. Rhinehart said I can't be exercising too much no more. Says my blood pressure is too high because of all the food I eat.

I do love to eat.

At some point, when I was eating so much, I could only feel the shape of the food because it got difficult to find the flavor. I'm not in the best shape. You'd need a lot of marble to make a statue out of me.

She handed me the bundle of bananas. "Anything else?"

I stood there frozen. I realized that this may be the last time I saw this little market. They had already bulldozed the house and built an intoxicant shop. My school was gone. Things were always being torn down so new things could be built and then eventually torn down. Things don't live for very long. The little market was the oldest thing I knew. And I started to feel like this place wasn't right. Like I was a fish that was taken out of a pond and put into a tank with clay pots and fake plants.

This was home, but not really a home.

This felt like a constructed exhibit.

She looked at me with concerned eyes after I stood mute for a few seconds.

"Are you okay?"

"Just a bit stressed."

She furrowed her brow for a moment.

"I see. Do you need a release?"

I hesitated for a bit. Then asked, "Do you need one too?"

"I could use one, yes."

"Okay. You can walk back with me.

Back at the register, I paid for my bananas. As she typed on the keyboard, I couldn't help but look at her. Her hair was thick. Her lips were plump. Her neck was delicate and slender. I looked too long because she looked back at me and said, "I'm not a robot. I don't think they made them this good yet."

"That's good to hear. They will get that good soon."

"Yes, they will."

She told me her name was Annette. Then she grabbed her purse and we left the market together, making our way back to my micro-dwelling.

~

"Are you ready?" Annette asked.

She came out of the bathroom and caught me looking at Momma's record player. I felt a jolt of pain in my chest. I didn't respond. She suggested I play some music. I told her I threw out all the records.

"Oh."

"I just couldn't hear any of them anymore, so I got rid of them."

"I see."

"Momma's not around anymore. That's just how it is. When it's their time to expire, it's what happens."

There was a tense silence, then Annette spoke up.

"Should we just get to it, then?"

Annette undressed herself then sat next to me on the couch. She was close to me now. Very close. I could feel the heat from her breath. She started stroking my hand. Hers were smooth like vanilla cream. She leaned over and pressed her lips onto mine. They were warm and plush, but she soon pulled herself back and gave me a strange look.

I didn't kiss her back.

"Are you alright?" she asked.

"Yes," I told her.

"Are you sure? You don't seem very into it."

"Into what?"

She raised one of her eyebrows.

"Okay, let's try this." She straddled me and pressed her lips back onto mine. This time more firm. She kept pressing her lips onto mine, and onto other parts of my face. She guided one of my hands onto her waist while she pressed her lips onto my neck. And she kept pressing and squeezing and stroking and it was all so much. Then she took herself back and looked into my eyes.

"Do you not feel me?" she asked.

"What?"

"Do you not feel me? Can you feel me?"

She patted my arm which rested on her waist. The fabric of her dress was soft. I nodded and she looked disappointed in me, like I had lied to her.

"You don't feel this?" She guided my hand inside her dress and onto her thigh. Her skin was soft and warm.

"Yes, I do feel this."

I could feel her, but I've felt enough people like her. Really, I felt nothing.

She started placing my hand on other areas of her body. They were all soft and warm. She kept repeating, asking if I could feel her until I stopped responding.

Her expression was blank, then worried.

"Are you okay?"

She started stroking my thigh, then started kissing me again. Everything went foggy for me, like I was trying to look through a plume of smoke. I saw a blurry kaleidoscope of shapes and colors, and I started to remember my first sun after my procedure. It peeked over the horizon and made the sky pink. I remember thinking to myself, "The sky is so beautiful it can't be real."

And that thought came into my head again as my thigh was being stroked and a pair of plush lips were resting on mine.

I pulled my face away from her.

"Do you ever think about this place?" I said with a bit of a tremble.

She gave me a confused look. "What do you mean?"

"Like . . ." My voice started to tense up. I was trying to find the right words. "Like . . . do you ever think that this place isn't right for you?"

"I'm sorry, I don't understand?"

Her hand reached my groin and I started to not care about the other things I wanted to ask her.

We enjoyed each other for a few hours. With the climactic endurance medication, I can go for a really long time. I always have some in case someone like Annette comes over.

We laid on the sofa for a bit after, then she got up and left, telling me she had to clean up the market.

I heard the door close, and I got up and looked out my small window. The balding man had his shades down, as did all the other residents in the complex.

I don't like to feel this way.

I turned off all the lights and sat back on my sofa to watch snippets on my floatscreen. I sat there and watched until my eyes hurt. Until they felt stripped of moisture. Until everything around me wasn't so cold and so quiet. And it was only a few hours later when I felt warm, and my eyelids couldn't stay open to watch the snippets any longer as they slowly covered everything.

I drifted into a sleep that made my stomach hurt, until my companion made a wind-chime sound.

Someone was at the door.

Assuming it was a delivery, I tapped a button on my companion and unlocked the door.

I closed my swollen eyes, trying to soothe myself into sleep. I heard footsteps coming up the stairs until I saw the figure standing at the doorway, covered by the dark. I wasn't startled. The figure had a familiar presence. I squished my eyes tight. It was someone I had not talked to in a long time.

She came closer.

I could see her face.

She looked distressed. Her eyes were sullen and defeated. And seeing her face all put together made my body weak, and my lips quivered enough to not let any words pass through them.

"Mordy?" Ellie said in a soft tone. She approached me on the coach and took my chin in her palm. "Oh, Mordy. Look what they've done to you." She wrapped her arms around me and started to cry. I put my arms around her and my body started shaking.

"I miss you," I mumbled into her head of hair.

She squeezed me harder, not wanting to let go. I felt a sharp pang in my chest. My eyes started to well up with tears, sitting on the cusp of the ducts until they dropped down my cheeks. They were so swollen from the snippets, it hurt to keep them open, but I wanted to look at her forever.

"Mordy," Ellie said with such a soothing, delicate voice. "Mordy, Mordy, Mordy. It's okay. It's okay."

Small beads of water glided down my cheeks. I didn't like this feeling. I *hated* this feeling. It's so cold and so quiet. I want to be mummy-wrapped in my bedsheets. I want to hear the singing and taste the rice pudding. I want a soft, gentle hand to caress me. I kept crying so I covered my eyes with my palms.

"They keep our thinking as deep as a puddle and our eyes as blind as a bull," Ellie said, stroking my face. "The flowers used to bloom until the flowers weren't needed anymore. Real green reduced to a distant memory."

My lips finally let words come out of them. "Why are you talking like this?" I asked her in between wet hiccups.

Her eyes were red and puffy now and looked like they were about to water, but she tightened her face and they stayed dry. From the bag slung over her shoulder, she pulled out a small, tattered book.

"I finally read it," she said. "I *finally* read it. I understand it now." She covered my delicate hands with hers. We shared the same supple skin. "I want to get rid of them, Mordy. I want to remove my shackles."

She looked down at my frail wrists. "And it looks like they tightened yours. Maybe a bit too tight."

I didn't say anything. I was holding myself back from tears, trying to keep my cheeks dry.

"I never opened it," Ellie said gently. "Not even once after you gave it to me. All those years it was sitting in Momma's house, collecting dust. Then I got it from the automated estate process when Momma passed. Then I opened it."

I couldn't say anything. I couldn't control my mouth. I just wanted to stand there and let the liquid gush from my eyes.

"It's time for us to go," she said. "It's time for us to leave."

"I can't go. I can't, I can't."

Sam Calvo

Ellie looked into my eyes, and I think she saw something hollow because she seemed to be taken back by my response.

"You're not like everyone else in this city who can't feel. When was the time where everyone could feel? When was that? God, there never was a time."

I let out a few wet hiccups.

"I don't know."

"I know a path to the lookout. We can make it out. It's time for us to leave."

"Leave? Leave where? Where are we going? What are we leaving?"

I was overwhelmed with emotion. Then Ellie put her tender hands around my face, kissed my forehead, then looked into my eyes.

"It's time for us to leave Macrosanti."

I'm Lying About Everything All The Time

An essay by Marcus Shelby

Except right now.

This is an exception I made for this essay.

But in all other cases, *I'm lying about everything all the time.*

Make a note of that.

First, I need an extension of my lunch break. I can only write so much and only be so creative in the thirty minutes they give me.

I never eat anyway.

I rarely have the appetite.

Working with the disturbed does that to a man.

I'm sitting at the desk they let me set up in the old storage closet in the basement. They even gave me a key with a happy face sticker on it. It's nice because I don't see happy faces around here.

I'm not allowed to hang anything on the walls but they didn't say anything about desk decor so sitting beside me, emanating a dim, orange light, is a salt lamp I got from some spiritual woman who read the palms of my hands and said that good fortune awaited me in my future.

Well, when the hell is that future?

When is my good fortune coming?

It better be soon because I've been trying to finish this ungodly story for some time now. The story itself is sewage, the elements feel as fake and as boring as imitation mahogany, and I'm struggling with a writer's block so massive, I'm convinced there's a malignant tumor pressing on the left hemisphere of my brain.

I want to snap this pen in half that I keep twirling around my fingers. I want to grab something and twist it and wring it and pull it as hard as I can. I want these perfect words to spill out of me already, like I'm dangling an old shoe I wore at the beach upside down to get all the bits of sand out.

But I'm not completely desperate, and my eyes haven't totally fallen out of their sockets, and my spine hasn't completely bent in the wrong direction. I cobbled together a draft, a sort of disgusting Frankenstein story, and submitted it to ninety-seven publications and magazines.

None of them liked it.

Here's a letter I received from one of them:

Dear Mr. Shelby,

Thank you for sending us your story. We appreciated the chance to read it. Unfortunately, we're going to pass on this one.

I really love the voice of this piece and your inventive terminology. I especially liked "snippets" and "floatscreen." And his quest for bananas was great. It's a really different kind of dystopian piece.

Unfortunately, I can't put my finger on what this piece needs. You have many good elements, but I think this needs a more interesting element for the reader to connect with, something that should excite the character but doesn't. Just my opinion, however. I think you can do better with such a wonderful setting and voice.

All the best,

Jonathan Laird
Editor, The Rusted Pen

What garbage!

Do they not know who I am?

Have their ears never been titillated by the name *Marcus Shelby*?

My words were scintillating on the pages I sent him. My metaphors perfectly executed, my story structure carefully built, and he has the audacity to tell me it's not *interesting*?

I grab a package of Ho Hos® from a box sitting under my desk and let the cream-filled, chocolatey tube massage the taste buds on my tongue. Why the hell did I say it like that? Why didn't I just say "I ate the Ho Ho®?"

I like eating processed treats like Ho Hos® and Zingers® and Twinkies® when I'm stressed because they're packed with anti-nauseant ingredients so you can eat a lot of them without puking. At least I think that's true because I've already eaten a dozen packages and my stomach hasn't rumbled once.

I guess today I have an appetite.

Kridan knocks twice on the door, signaling to me that my next shift would be with disturbed on the fifth floor. In the beginning, when I requested a desk and a quiet space I could use to write during my lunch, Kridan would knock twice, then barge in and tell me that my next shift was with disturbed, which was enough time to hide my writing under the desk but was nonetheless a dangerous situation. He can't find out about my writing, nor can anyone else here. I told him, as well as everyone else, that I used the room to meditate, which was understandable given the stressful work we do. I told Kridan that when he barged in, it broke my concentration, so now he just knocks twice on the door to let me know I'm working with the disturbed. He never barges in anymore.

I never planned on being an orderly in a psych ward. It just happened this way. I really wanted to be a screenwriter, but people said I wrote things that were too dark and terrifying and sinister. Well, I write things like this because my head is full of things that are terrifying and sinister. "Why can't the girl fall in love with the boy instead of cutting off his fingers?" people would say, and to them I'd say that the fingers represent touch, sensation, and connection, and that those themes were blatantly shown throughout the story. They never understood.

Maybe I was being too pompous. You must understand that it's in the nature of writers to act pompous—to think that everything they touch is a masterpiece. To believe that their work is as groundbreaking as Shakespeare or Flaubert or Steinbeck. They think they're clever, shrewd, perceptive, witty, astute individuals who have created their own membership in some faux intelligentsia nobody cares about. They think of themselves as great revealers of truth, like a diamond miner unearthing a shiny, polished stone from a heap of dirty soil.

To state it firmly—writers are naturally, wholeheartedly pompous. They're obsessed, arrogant, egotistical, self-flagellating and self-affirming perfectionists who tend to have disagreeable characteristics, but want to, in the purest form, *change the way people see the world*. And it is this characteristic, coupled with the others that I had previously listed, that have produced the greatest stories, fantasies, fables, essays, and poems ever created.

So, on the topic of the egoism and pompousness of writers—and in my dutiful attempt to procrastinate on finishing my own story—I'd like to share a few reasons why I write, because the best cure that I've found for writer's block is writing.

Reason 1:
The Power of the Written Word

I have very firm beliefs about the power of the novel, more importantly, the written word.

The purpose of art, at least to me, is to collapse the machinery in your head that makes you think a certain way, or to at the very least knock a few screws loose so that the whole system can eventually come crumbling down.

Using the gift of our shared language, our mutual, invariably spoken agreement on certain words and their percise meanings, we can wrap people in our beautiful, made up world. And we use these agreed words to trigger images in people's heads about this made up world. I can write about a blue house with a large chimney that sits on a lake. Right now, we are both thinking of a house that's blue with a rather large chimney that's near a lake, but the house that you're thinking of and the house that I'm thinking of are vastly different.

One of the reasons I write novels instead of producing plays or films is because I believe the greatest medium of art is one that can bring the subjectivity of its material down to the individual experience. The uniqueness of people, the complexity that comprises a person's being, make it impossible for two people to ingest a novel in the exact same way. There are an infinite number of ways of interpreting the world, and the written word is tantamount to upholding those interpretations.

Another reason, a negligible one, is the operational expense. The cost for writing a story about a three horned, fire-breathing dragon with emerald scales that attacks a castle with an impenetrable gate armed with bow-wielding elves at the helm is much cheaper than the cost of doing the same on the cinema screen. See, you just imagined the three-horned dragon plunging its way toward the castle with a molten jet of fire shooting from its mouth.

And I got you to do all of that for free.

Reason 2:
Obsession with Legacy

Everything I write right now can be worth as much as gold or as worthless as dust, depending on how others value it, or better yet, how I value it.

The latter is the key here.

What words of mine will remain when my mouth becomes unable to speak?

Will they be held in books that free imprisoned minds and spur people to think creatively, to love and care for others, to sacrifice when needed to and to cherish what they didn't think was important? Or will they be used as paperweights? As doorstops? As antique decor in a futuristic antiseptic living room with furniture made of molten gel and walls built with self-healing concrete?

I'm insatiably critical of myself, continuously practicing this wicked art until it leads to self-abatement. Usually, it's thinking that I can write something better, that my words can be more clever, that my truths can be less shrouded and more pronounced. This will create a vicious, never-ending loop like a snake trying to swallow its own tail, and it never leads to anything productive, but understanding this notion doesn't stop the self-criticism.

There's literature, sitting on a gilded pedestal, then there's my little chicken scratch, no more pleasant to look at than graffiti on a gas station bathroom wall, no more titillating than a flickering bulb in a dusty lamp, no more inspiring than a barren wasteland of severed tree trunks. The beautiful literature that stuffs the library shelves is written with beautiful ink—with pens that have feathers or diamonds or orbs filled with liquid creativity instead of erasers, while my little, dinky, worthless scribblings are written with the lead of a dull pencil or the sticky, dusty keys on the keyboard of an old laptop, one that has been dropped on concrete, slammed repeatedly with an angry fist, and spilled on with various drinks.

We love to fill our heads with this nonsense, and while it may be true in a temporal sense, it is not eternally true. That should give solace to anyone who decides to create good art.

It is important to note that my obsession with legacy rides a tandem bike with my fear of disappearance—that who I was am a person will eventually flicker out. That when I die, in the minds of my peers, the memories they have of me will be as retrievable as a nice pair of shoes they once had. At some point, despite whether you've created what the collective public deems "transformative art" or not, people will remember you as long as what you create is true to yourself. That is important to reiterate to yourself every once in a while before it gets lost in a sea of criticism.

Reason 3:
Understand Myself and Endure the Suffering

Writing helps me be in tune with myself, and to endure the eternal suffering of the world by bracing myself as much as possible.

If the world is a burning house—maybe a blue house with a large chimney that sits by a lake—then writing is dousing my mind with fire-retardant.

Let me explain.

I worked a few jobs before I became an orderly.

First, I was a grocery clerk. Then a line cook for a few months and after that, a maintenance worker at a retirement home. I never wanted to work at a retirement home, but my court-ordered psychiatrist thought it'd be a good idea.

"It'll calm you down to see how they live such simple, relaxed lives," he said to me. "It'll keep your troubled mind from escalating further. There's not much stimulation there. And after a few months, if the director tells me that you've been an exceptional employee, we can even talk about weaning you off your medication."

I guess you need a bit of context here: when I was a child I was pronounced insane by the same ward where I now work. I was given medication, and a psychologist who, even to this day as an adult, I sometimes still see.

I assume you now probably want to know why I was pronounced insane.

Well, I don't know.

I had what they called "bad school performance." I was throwing temper tantrums and locking myself in my room and showing signs of "dissociative behavior." That's what was written on the psychiatric reports when I was first admitted to the ward, but those fancy psychiatric reports don't tell you about my mom.

My mom believed in God.

She owned a knit shop in Waddica.

She chain-smoked nine coffin nails a day.

And she didn't quite understand that during those nineteen years of nail burning—whether it was while she sat on the couch or outside on the porch or in the car while I sat in my carseat in the back—she was actually laying in a coffin, waiting to die as the nails were slowly hammered in, tightening the cover that sealed the thing shut, not letting the air escape as she kept inhaling garbage and exhaling toxic smoke, which lingered in that tightly shut coffin until it choked her.

But before the smoke constricted her weak, feeble lungs, she would say the most awful things to me. She would tell me to stop ruining her life by simply existing and that she had to like me because I came out of her. "You're supposed to be successful and save us from this shithole they call an apartment," she'd yell at me when I brought home a failed report card, which was followed by a deep inhale from the coffin nail crutched between her two fingers. "That's why I had you in the first place."

I can't even call them what they really are. I don't want to. I like to imagine that they really were coffin nails.

I lived in a small town, so eventually everyone knew I was insane so it was quite difficult to find a job that allowed me to do any serious work, as in, work that could damage the company if any of my insane tendencies crept out of me. Because of my poisoned mind, I was trapped in perpetual, remedial, work. Work that made me stare at the hands of clocks, count the blemishes on tiled floors, and sit on the toilet in bathrooms long enough for my legs to go numb. I did all of this on a daily basis at all of my previous jobs.

Then I saw a job advertisement to work at the psych ward and thought it would be a good opportunity to work with people who cure poisoned minds like mine.

Maybe I could better understand my own, I thought.

Kridan hired me as an orderly, helping the disturbed with their clothes and moving them between exam rooms and giving them baths. On occasion, I would also help or assist during activities or supervise during quiet time.

I still can't believe they let me be an orderly.

It's like having a murderer as a prison guard.

At first, I wanted to be around people who helped the ones with poisoned minds. I saw the job at the psych ward as a way to do that.

Maybe these people could fix what's inside of me?

Wow, how naive I was!

This place is horrific. The things they do to these people are barbaric. They keep them trapped and domesticated like sedated dogs, stripped of free will and a clear mind. They keep them poisoned, if you can believe that. There's no money in perfectly adjusted, self-aware, and self-sustaining individuals. If everyone was like that, then the director might as well surround this place with dynamite and reduce it to rubble.

But after some time, when I realized that this place was a prison instead of a haven, a new thought popped in my head: *Maybe I can fix what's inside of me.*

That's when I started writing. I wrote all my thoughts. The good ones and the bad ones. I kept track of the things I wrote. I wrote about why I wrote about certain things. Why did I write that? Why did I write it that way?

Writing was all I ever did on my lunch breaks. I sat in bathroom stalls, writing on scraps of paper for a year until I mustered the courage to ask for the basement space to meditate.

I was writing for myself. Writing out all my thoughts. Spilling them on blank pages. I hated seeing a page with nothing on it, so I filled it with words. And the words soon started to speak to me, as if that poisoned mind of mine was trying to talk to me. Eventually it did. It did a good job at that.

Writing has become a tool to fortify my mind, to stare at a blank page and try to find the words that are buried deep inside of me. tT write them as elegantly and as coherently as I can has allowed me to understand myself deeper than any other way.

As rewarding as writing is, and how much I love creating stories, like the one I'm struggling to write right now, so many times I've wanted to give up. I sometimes feel that I am trapped in my own head when in reality, my head is trapped in me. Somehow, it's been able to imprison me from the inside.

To put it bluntly: people who have not braced themselves for the world will soon have no desire to live in it. Death is a terrifying state to many, and a welcoming virtue to some. Death nullifies your suffering, as well as everything else that you ever knew. Life is suffering, and I have chosen to endure it today by being alive.

But don't worry: at some point, we all die after suffering from some terrible illness. You just can't see mine through a microscope.

Reason 4:
To Change the Way People See the World

To state it firmly—writers are obsessed, arrogant, egotistical, self-flagellating and self-affirming perfectionists who tend to have disagreeable characteristics, but want to, in the purest form, *change the way people see the world.*

Writing is an art I love.

And through my art, I want to reform humanity.

I say this with bravado: we must strive to produce art to create a vision, not stimulate a behavior. Programs and propaganda stimulate behavior. Art designs a new vision for the world, one that can breathe on its one or fly without the aid of others. A vision will spawn behaviors that align with that vision. Behaviors without a proper vision are just arbitrary marching orders.

How it bemoans me to read a book or see a play or watch a film about someone who's homeless, and about all the problems that come with being homeless, and how awful it is to be homeless, and by the end, I find myself saying, "Something needs to be done to help them!" Then after a few minutes, that thought dissipates like a fine mist as I waddle over to the refrigerator in my heated apartment and grab a can of pomegranate-flavored water and sit on my couch propped up with pillows stuffed with feathers that were plucked from a goose.

If a piece of art about the homeless compels you to volunteer, donate food, or give money the next time you see someone holding a cardboard sign by a stop light, but you still see the dirtiness and smell the trash on them, then to me, *it is not beautiful art.* But if a piece of art can construct a vision of wiping away the dirtiness we see on these people, then to me, *it is beautiful art.*

I want to create a new vision through my writing.

But words are dangerous. The thoughts that come from words are dangerous. The actions that come from thoughts are dangerous. Our words create peace but they also cause bloodshed. Our words nurture and enlighten but they also cheat and deceive. They make people sane just as much as they make people insane. I always worry about making people crazy. I want to relieve people from the crazy rather than make them crazy. J.D. Salinger must've believed the same thing.

Just because a writer wants to change the way people see the world, doesn't mean they want to make a change for the good. As much as we want to believe it to be true, writers are not born with pleasant virtues. They, like everybody else, must be molded with them. For the egotistical, self-absorbed writer, it's better to be remembered as a noble than a tyrant. There are more statues of nobles than tyrants and the statues of tyrants that are erected are eventually taken down, or at the very least, perpetually coated in a dense layer of spit.

I am one who wants to make a change for the good.

I realized that after I'd seen what this institution was doing to the disturbed. I wanted to write stories that could aid in freeing themselves from their shrouded servitude.

I remember a while back, we were running immersion experiments on this disturbed girl. She was mute. She didn't speak. She had experienced something horrific. Something that wouldn't make you want to say anything else forever. Even the guy she was with was trying to take care of her, until he gave up and left, taking their infant daughter with him.

Kridan explained that we were trying to remove the painful memories of her friends so that hopefully she could live a normal life. We were always short on staff so Kridan had me there to help with the fluid bags after her immersions. Her chart said she was twenty-seven, but her face was wrinkled with skin that hung dead without care. This place was aging her, slowly killing her.

Her mother frequently came in to comfort her. And Kridan would feed her these lies. "We need to do another immersion," he'd say in that hackneyed, quasi-comfortoning tone to her. And as someone who may at any moment become a bereaved mother, either clutching her pearls or stroking her daughter's feeble hand, she would cave in and allow the immersions to take place.

They never worked. I'm not a doctor or a nurse but I've seen the charts. They never worked—but boy, were they expensive. As is everything else in this place. To Kridan, there was always a chance that the immersion would work until one day, the girl's mother opened her purse to find nothing but cobwebs and dust. Then he'd declare that the immersions won't work. I promise you that.

Thankfully, she didn't have to go broke for the immersions to stop working. One day, they were trying to remove the memories and her optic chiasm got in the way, so we ended up making her blind and mute. We stopped the immersions after that and sent her home.

I wish she could have freed herself. I think the immersions had vaporized whatever free will was left in her head. She was such a beautiful woman. I could see it under all those wrinkles.

You must understand that everyday, there are people trapped in programs with invisible handcuffs. And the sinister part of these programs is their camouflage. They walk and talk like visions, leading the people they infect to believe that the program is as natural as the petals on a flower. This is a facade, and it's one of the most important reasons why I'm writing these stories.

I really do think she would have liked the story I'm writing right now. That beautiful girl, along with all the other patients here, motivate me to finish my stories in hopes that they may read them and find solace, safety, and understanding, and to ultimately, as is my intention, see the vision I have created so that they may free themselves from programs that have polluted their minds.

But nobody will publish my books.

And I don't care.

I'll print the pages and bind them together myself.

I'll use a fake last name so nobody will know it's me.

Maybe I'll even put a copy or two in the book carts they keep in the Leisure Rooms so hopefully, a patient will read it and find the world a little more bearable. A little more gentle. A little more pleasant, as a change in their vision will allow them to see the world this way.

I'm writing these stories that touch me, and I'm making them up as I go.

Remember: *I'm lying about everything all the time.*

And I've never had so much fun lying.

And I've never spoken so much truth by lying.

But this truth will never be understood by anyone because my writing is so terrible, so egregiously awful that I don't think it will connect with a single soul, let alone spur anyone to open the novel itself. And I'll stay imprisoned in my mind forever.

Sorry, that's the insatiable criticism speaking.

Or it isn't.

I can't tell anymore.

Kridan just knocked five times on the door, which means I'm late for my shift.

Oh, well. Until the next time I tend to my chicken scratch.

Sincerely,

Marcus Shelby

Addison's Wake

January 12th

Dear Mom,

Please help me.

I don't know who you are or even where you are, but I need you to help me.

Dad told me you exist.

He told me that you were around before I could even get my feet under myself to walk. He told me you held me in your arms when I came out of you, and that I was the most beautiful thing you'd ever seen. It's hard to believe Dad sometimes, but I want to believe that this is true.

That I am your daughter.

I am writing this letter to you from a place of horror. I hope it reaches you fast enough for you to get me out of this place. Dad dropped me off here today after he got fed up with me for the last time. He told the front desk that I was unfixable. He was ashamed to take me anywhere, and that he was sick of taking care of disableds, so he dropped me here to live with all the other sick kids.

Next thing I knew, the strong men in white suits dressed like door-to-door milkmen took me under my armpits and I started thrashing around. They didn't know what to do with me and I don't know what to do with myself. I don't like people touching me like that, it feels so sick. I thrashed around so they fit me in a heavy jacket that bound my arms around my back and tied me to the radiator in some room until I calmed myself down.

I didn't calm myself down. The air around me felt so thin. Everything felt so scary. I kept yelling for the white suits. I told them I had to use the bathroom, but they never answered, so I just laid on the floor, tied to the radiator in a sour-smelling puddle of my own embarrassment.

When I stopped thrashing, they untied me and let me get ready to sleep. There isn't an available bed for me yet, so they make me sleep in an empty room on a mattress thin enough for my bones to feel the cold concrete floor below it. I don't have a pillow and I'm crying. I pulled a loose piece of paper from my bag and started writing this letter to you.

I don't want to be here. I wrote the name of the ward on the back of this letter. Please come save me from this awful place.

Love,
Addison

January 14th

Dear Mama,

I hope you don't mind it if I call you Mama. It feels like what I would have called you if you were around.

The last two days have been horrible.

They left me alone in that tiny room all day with that filthy thin mattress. But today, they finally found an open bed for me in the main room. They also let me mingle with the other sick kids in the ward.

During Leisure Time, a lot of them played cards and board games. Others stayed put like marble statues. One girl sat lifeless in a chair that faced the window, which looked out to a plain of dead grass. Another girl was snapping her fingers at some fixed point in space. Her name is Millie. At night, she pulled the covers all the way over her head and curled herself up like a frightened puppy.

I walked around the Recreation Room. A girl dressed in an oversized red sweater with a missing front tooth started yelling at me. Freak atheist activist! she kept saying to me like they were the only three words her raspy voice let her say.

Freak atheist activist!

Freak atheist activist!

She kept going at me for a bit, then waddled to an isolated corner in the leisure room and mumbled something incoherent to herself.

Edward was the first sick kid I talked to. He was older than me. Old enough to drive a car at least. He sat at a plastic table playing cards with a few other sick kids. He had piercing blue eyes and wispy blonde hair that stuck up so high it looked like he had been zapped by a cattle prod. I walked up and said hi.

He asked me why I was in here and I told him Dad dropped me off. He scoffed and said Dad was never coming back. The other sick boys didn't say anything. They kept to their cards. I wanted to retreat to the large couch in the middle of the room but it started to melt so I asked Edward to teach me a game, but he refused.

You're too looney to play cards games, I can see it in your eyes, he said to me.

And that made me really sad until one of the sick kids, a girl with red hair, freckles, and rosy cheeks, started hollering at Edward, saying he was being rude as hell to me. Edward swatted at the air near her, but she kept hollering at him. Edward told her to leave him alone, but she started swinging at him, and Edward started swinging back until the white suits came in and took them both away. The freckled girl with her legs kicking the air and Edward who went limp as a dead fish. I didn't see them for the rest of the day.

We then had a session of music therapy where we all laid on our backs and listened to some relaxing music. Millie started screaming something fierce and two white suits had to carry her out like she was a dusty old carpet. The rest of us laid on that floor, dead like hollow caskets for the rest of the hour.

A lot of us have trouble acting right so to keep order, we all get some sort of medicine here. The nurses give us little pills that we swallow with a paper cup of water. Then we open our mouths to the nurses to let them know we took the medicine because some of the kids cheat. Some of the kids have so much medicine in them that their limbs get stiff like blocks of wood, sitting motionless for hours as they drool from their mouths.

I took the medicine too, Mama. I'm one to follow the rules, I promise you that! I promise to follow all the rules once you come and get me.

Oh, the rest of the day was so awful and full of nothingness. Just time for me to sit and deal with my own existence. No wonder all the kids in here are loony. They're trapped here. Forced to live with their poisoned heads. And Dad says my head is poisoned too like these sick kids, but I promise I'm a good kid. I promise.

At night, it gets awfully lonely. It's so dark in this giant room they all put us in to sleep, like rows of cattle. I sometimes crack open my eyes to watch Joe the janitor mopping the floors and emptying the garbage cans. One time, he caught me with my eyes open and didn't say anything. He just smiled and kept mopping the floor. I like Joe. He's a really sweet guy.

All the windows have steel bars over them, but an adorable squirrel managed to squeeze through the one near my bed. He burrowed himself in my blankets and we said goodnight to each other. I've never had a pet. I always wanted a puppy, but Dad said I couldn't even take care of a blind fish, but if I had a pet, I'd name it Jambo. So that is what I called my new squirrel friend.

Jambo.

Love,
Addison

January 15th

Dear Mama,

I hope you're on your way.
Things are not getting better.
This place is humiliating.
I'm new and I don't like the feeling. I don't know all the rules yet and I have a hard time understanding. Sometimes my brain gets messed up.

During Leisure Time, I asked one of the white suits if I could go for a walk. He looked at me and said sure, and pointed to a hallway door. I tried to open the door but it was locked. He told me I needed a key. I asked him where I could find the key and he told me he had the key, and that he would use it to open that door when it was Recreation Time. He laughed at me, and so did a few of the other white suits. I felt so ashamed. You have no idea how mad I was at them, Mama. I wanted to ball my fists and punch him so bad, but I knew I couldn't do that. I thought this place was supposed to help me.

I didn't do much during Leisure Time. I just sat on the melting couch in the middle of the room. On the wall, there's a big bronze plaque that lists all the reasons for admission. I read a few of them:

Hysteria
Novel Reading
Laziness

Grief
Epileptic Fits
Brain Fever
Over Stimulation of Mind
Intellectually Feeble
Immoral Life
Female Disease

Close to the end of Leisure Time, I saw an interesting book sitting in the book cart. It looked like it was put together by hand. It didn't look like any of the other books, so I grabbed it and started reading, but I could only read a few pages before Leisure Time ended.

We then had music therapy again. This time we listened to some lovely jazz music. While I was lying on my back on the cold concrete floor with all the other sick kids, a door opened and a pair of feet shuffled inside. The girl laid down right beside me. She was the red-haired girl who was hollering and swinging at Edward yesterday. She had a few bruises on her arm.

Edward walked in shortly after with a ring of purple around his right eye.

N'body should be talkin' to you like that, she whispered to me while the soft jazz music filled the room like a husky fog. 'Nbody should be treated like that.

Her name was Margot, and we were together a lot after that. After she stood up for me and all. You know I would've stood up for myself, Mama, but I was so new and scared and didn't know any better.

Margot showed me around. All the different games to play, where to find the best seats in the Recreation Room to watch the small TV that hung in the corner, and what to avoid at the breakfast buffet (oatmeal and cottage cheese). We talked a lot to each other while we waited in line for food. We talked about our love for jazz, how badly some of the boys smelled, and the awful food they served us.

It all looks like gruel, she said to me, and it doesn't get better. Margot told me one time she flung a heap of it with her spoon onto the wall and it splattered all over the place. She got the straitjacket and a sedative for three days for doing that.

And we'd talk for a long time.

We'd about everything we knew. We even talked about family. Margot's parents didn't want her just like Dad didn't want me. One day, they just dropped her off then let their car tires kick up rocks as they drove away. She tried calling home many times, but someone else answered each time. Margot's been here nearly two years, and not a single letter or phone call came from her family.

I might'swell give up, she keeps saying to herself.

And two years is a long time. Long enough to know things, ya know? I asked Margot today while waiting in line for breakfast if there was anything good in this place. She lifted her upper lip to reveal a row of rotten teeth.

The only good thing in here is the dental care, she said to me.

And I couldn't believe she'd been in here so long. She's a tough one, Mama, I'll say that. I think you'd really like her if you two ever met. Maybe when you come pick me up, she can come too. She'd be awfully excited to have someone who cares about her.

The rest of the day got ahead of me and just went by without letting me know. Now I'm lying in my bed among the other cattle.

I can't sleep and the moon hurts.

I got up from my bed and looked out one of the windows, pressing my head against the cold bars that covered it. The trees outside were swaying and the grass was being tickled by the wind in this godforsaken place in the middle of nowhere.

And now I realize that you need to come quickly to not only save me, but also Margot.

Love,
Addison

January 16th

Dear Mama,

I really hope you're on your way. You must've already read my first letter and jumped in your car. You'll probably be here soon, but I do still like to write, so I'll keep writing to you, Mama.

Edward agreed to teach me a game during Leisure Time after he finished fiddling with his sheets of paper. It was called blackjack, and Margot stood right near him as he dealt out the cards and slowly taught me the game. I bet he felt her breath tickle the back of his bare neck when she stood there. I don't think he once thought of swatting his hand at her. He already didn't like that nasty purple ring around his eye. Margot and I thought he looked funny, like a wimpy pirate.

Then we had lunch in the mess hall.

While we waited in line, Margot and I talked about Cottage Lake where we both grew

up, the juicy blue cheeseburgers from Scooter's,
and the annoying pan flute band that played at
the Hillside Mall every Sunday. Margot said she
always wanted to grab one of those flutes
from their mouths and snap it over her knee. We
also talked about what kind of disgusting animal
Edward would be if he were to be one. We
agreed on a possum. One that lived in a
dumpster.

The kitchen staff gave us our trays of
gruel, a gross, gray sludge in a bowl, a few pieces
of bread, and a celery stick. A few kids started
eating immediately. One girl swayed back and
forth. Another held her neck while walking in
circles. Edward hollered about how he can't eat
celery sticks anymore. Margot looked down at
her gruel and clenched her fists, whitened her
knuckles, and made her face go almost pink with
rage. She wanted to blow up but restrained
herself after a few seconds, then started to
eat.

I looked down at my tray and my slush of
lunch gruel had become a bloody salmon, which I

started stabbing with my fork. I did that for probably two minutes.

It was so hideous I wanted it to die, Mama.

I kept looking at the clock because I know the clock is real and it keeps ticking. I don't even like salmon.

Salmon is better than squirrel, Jambo said to me as he sat pleasantly by the windowsill, feeding on a walnut.

I wanted to tell Jambo that he should try the gruel for himself if he was so sure, but he leapt outside before I could. Margot and I pray before each meal that they'll put out just one food that won't make us throw up so we can just eat that every day.

I've tried calling Dad, but he doesn't answer. And I've decided to stop calling him. How I hate him so much. How revolting I think he is. I hope I never have to hear him call me Dolly again.

I really hope you answer these letters, and know that I would call you in a heartbeat if I knew your number.

I promise you that, Mama.

I promise you that.

Love,
Addison

January 25th

Dear Mama,

I'm sorry it's been some time.

The white suits found my pen and pieces of paper in my bag and took them away from me, leaving me with only my clothes and a toothbrush with a thumbprint handle so I couldn't hurt myself with it.

I was really worried that I wouldn't be able to write to you, but Edward knew a way to get a pen and some sheets of paper for me from the nurse's office (I have to give him my canteen money for the next week). Now I keep my pen and sheets of loose paper under my mattress and only write at night when it's safe.

And I don't know why they took my pen and papers away from me. The nurses say the pen is dangerous and that all feelings should be expressed in group therapy with the others. Oh, yeah. I started participating in group therapy. I guess they don't make you start doing that in the beginning if you get strapped to the radiator and wet yourself. They want to wean you in.

The psychologist mostly talks and only a few sick kids speak up about anything. If any, one or two will say a few sentences, then the rest of the hour is spent sitting in silence.

The only kids that ever really talk are Mallory, who tried to slit her wrists to be with her mother, and of course Edward, who never says anything worth more than diddly squat.

One time he went on a long rant about how his favorite baseball team (the Bears? The Jets? God if I even remember) was cheated out of a World Series a few years ago, and I sat there wishing Margot was there to put a purple ring around his other eye.

The white suits also thought I'd now be able to start doing 'therapeutic chores' like cleaning the public washrooms and sweeping the floor of the Recreation Room. It's grunt work. The nurses say it helps us adjust to normal living, that it gives us responsibility, but I'm just angry about it all the time. I'm on my hands and knees all day, scrubbing what looks like dried-up pieces of cereal on a dirty bathroom floor. I hate it so much.

After my chores, I was able to read more of my book during Leisure Time. I felt so connected to the characters. They were both trapped like me, trying to find a way to escape a horrific place. And I really hope they do. I really do hope they escape, Mama.

Sam Calvo

After Leisure Time, I met up with Margot at the cafeteria for lunch. She didn't have to do the therapeutic chores because they say she's too aggressive.

They're worried I'd snap off the mop handle and start swinging at the white suits, she joked.

We were served our lunch gruel and both of us looked down at our trays. They decided not to serve food that doesn't make us want to puke, so we ate our gruel, then went to music therapy where we both laid on the floor as Pink Floyd filled the room.

The rest of the day slowly got away from me, like it was a bottle of water with a tiny little hole at the bottom, letting just a little bit of liquid out at a time. I felt heavy all day like I was weighed down in a tub of molasses. Then I blinked and suddenly the windows were all dark and the sun had retreated behind the countryside.

I got in my bed among the other rows of beds. I draped the thin blanket over my whole

≈ 185 ≈

body and I watched Jambo perch on the windowsill, nibbling on his tail. Mallory sleeps a few beds away from me and she started crying so a white suit came by with a sedative for her. The crying stopped. Everything was dark and I wanted to cry too but I didn't want the sedative. When they give me the sedative, my body feels like a defective container, and I hate the feeling. I hate it so much.

I hope you've been getting my letters, Mama. I fold each of them nicely and set them on the windowsill for Jambo to take them to the post office. He promised he'd deliver them, and that he'd tell the people at the post office to make sure they get to you. Maybe the mail takes longer than I thought, but I'll keep writing to you.

I only have a few sheets of paper and a leaky pen, but I will make sure my words cover every little bit of space I can fill on them. I will keep writing until you come here and take me away. Away is where home is for me.

Love,
Addison

January 26th

Dear Mama,

Why didn't Dad tell me? Why would he hide it from me? I couldn't believe it when I heard it. And I finally feel that I can find you.

I was mopping down the patient intake area and the nice old lady at the front desk started asking me lots of questions. Asked my name and where I was from and how I liked school and all the sorts. I don't like answering questions, Mama. I don't like to think about myself and then tell people about that stuff too much, but she kept going and going. She was the same woman that was there when Dad dropped me off. But after I told her all the things I let myself say out loud, she said it was a shame that I had to be committed to the same place my mom was.

THE SAME PLACE!

Mama, you didn't tell me you were also committed to this awful place! My God you must be on your way right now, driving over every godforsaken speed limit sign they put up so you can pull me out. I couldn't believe it when she said it. I still don't believe it, but she had a truthfulness to her voice that I couldn't ignore.

Mama, you're like me!

You're also sick!

What was it like?

How long were you here for?

I asked the front desk lady as many questions as I could but she couldn't answer any of them. It was such a long time ago but she recognized the last name. She said you were admitted to the adult ward down the street where she used to work and that you always mopped the floors in the waiting area. She said I also had the same little mole above my right lip, just like you.

Oh, Mama, you must be so beautiful with that little mole on your lip. I imagine you with beautiful hair, thick as can be, with plump, plushy cheeks like cumulus clouds and arms so delicate but so warming and sheltering that one could feel absolutely nothing but comfort when wrapped around them. And I can't wait for you to see me.

I'm gonna fold this letter with extra care, make sure the words I write look extra pretty, and tell Jambo to make extra sure that it gets delivered to the post office.

Mama. I can't wait for you to see how much I've grown and how beautiful I've become. Oh, how I can't wait for you to see me, Mama!

You're gonna be so happy to see me.

Love,
Addison

January 29th

Dear Mama,

I've been pretty glum recently.

The group therapy doesn't make the couch stop melting and the chores are anything but therapeutic. But while I wait here for you, I promised myself that I would do all that I could to get better. Margot has helped me a lot these past few days because she's trying herself to get better too, ya know. But it hasn't been going that way for her.

Her aggression's been getting worse.

Something on her lunch tray yesterday put her over the edge. She threw it against the wall and trapped herself in one of the isolation rooms. An army of white suits surrounded the door, trying to get in, but even with the keys, Margot's wrists were strong enough to hold the turning knob in place.

Finally with some verbal prodding from the nurses, she reluctantly opened the door to the room. The mirror was shattered and she stood there with a broken shard of glass in her hand.

Apparently, the white suits bull-charged her.

They were so afraid of her, she's so fierce, Mama. She went down fighting. They got the shard of glass from her but she was able to sink her teeth in the arm of one of the white suits. The shape of Margot's teeth must be implanted into that arm, knowing how hard she must've bitten.

After that, Margot stopped waiting in line with me. She stopped lying on the floor with me in music therapy. Now, she stays in her room all day. They keep her in there for safety, they say. Her food gets delivered to her and I rarely see her.

I was playing cards with Edward and he joked that Margot was gonna get the ice pick, which sounded mighty terrifying.

They use the ice pick to keep you alive, Edward said as he dealt cards around the table, but you stay alive like a sedated dog.

I don't like thinking about Margot as a sedated dog. The thought is really scary.

Better a sedated dog than a sedated squirrel, Jambo whispered to me as he laid comfortably on my thigh, his curled fluffy tail wrapped around himself.

I disagreed a lot with Jambo, but it was better to curb my pride instead of getting into an argument. If I started bickering with Jambo, I knew the white suits would strap me back in the jacket and tie me to a pole. Jambo gave me a concerned look and hopped off my lap and leapt out the window.

The moon is very bright tonight, Mama.
I hope you can see it.

Love,
Addison

Sam Calvo

January 30th

Dear Mama,

We had art therapy today.

We made stress paintings. They say it's
therapeutic. You paint what represents your
stress, then you're supposed to paint something
happy over it.

I painted the whole canvas a bright red.

I don't know why but it stressed me out
so much.

Then I drew a picture of you.

I tried my best! I added the little mole
right above your lip just like the old lady at the
front desk said. I also drew a little Jambo in
the corner. Edward drew some baseball players
whose names I didn't care to remember. Then
he looked over at my painting and started
making fun of your eyes, how they were lopsided
and all messed up. I wished Margot was there to
shut him up.

But I promise you Mama that I painted you the most beautiful way I could.

When you come pick me up, maybe they'll let me take the painting with me so you can see it for yourself.

One of the sick kids started hollering outta nowhere. I don't think he liked his painting because he started smacking the canvas with a paintbrush full of maroon. One of the white suits grabbed him and he started shouting more. Somethin's followin' us, somethin's followin' us! he kept yelling. He then let out some hiccupy cries and chattered his teeth like the room was walled in with blocks of ice. They got him out of the room and we all kept painting like nothing happened.

I met with a doctor today for the first time for an end-of-the-month evaluation. The doctor was surprised by my condition. He said it was extremely rare, but that doesn't make me feel any better. Do I get some stupid trophy for being rare? Does the doctor even care about that? I hope when you were here they didn't say anything awful like that to you, Mama. Treating you like a spider with nine legs, some grotesque marvel of science.

I didn't feel like doing anything for the rest of the day. I didn't play cards with Edward during Leisure Time and I didn't speak to anyone. I wanted to talk with Margot but they kept her locked away.

It made me really sad.

I went to bed as early as they allowed me to.

I didn't even care to see if Jambo was sitting on the windowsill, cleaning his paws.

You must be on your way by now, Mama.

I hope you are.

Love,
Addison

February 2nd

Dear Mama,

Margot got the ice pick yesterday.

They finally let her back in with the other sick kids for Leisure Time. Her head had a real nasty scar on it. They even took a big chunk of her hair too. She didn't speak and had a dimwitted smile on her face forever. She was drenched in sweat and shaking all the time. It's like she was turned into something primal. She lost whatever made her Margot.

I tried talking to her in the lunch line today but she just sat in her chair with a blanket over her knees, smiling. She had no thoughts, feelings, or emotions. She wasn't Margot anymore, and I know she was really trying hard to change. They didn't give her enough time! She was doing so well!

She didn't participate in art or music therapy and didn't hang around us anymore during Leisure Time. The nurses helped her up and made sure her blood flowed through her body, did some tango with her in what the white suits called "dancing for the deteriorated."

They took her away from me, Mama. How could they do that? Isn't this place supposed to cure us? Now I have night terrors and I sweat through my bedsheets. The nurses say it's normal but it's not. They lie. They all lie and they know it. They don't know what to do with us and they make up things for us to do because they think it'll help us be normal, like they know what normal is.

I thought about running away. Jambo mentioned trying to find a rock and slowly but surely every night I would break down the bars over the window until they crumbled, then I would run away from this godforsaken place, but it's so cold outside and the grass is beginning to gather frost and I don't have any warm clothes or sturdy shoes. I'd freeze to death out there.

I've sent so many letters to you, Mama. Have you gotten them? Please write back to me. I'm really scared this time. I know I've sent you a lot of letters, Mama, but I really hope you get this one. I'm gonna fold it extra, extra nice.

I just wish you came here sooner.
We could've saved her.
I just hope you can save me.
They gave up on Margot.
Dad gave up on me.
You must be on your way by now.
Please don't give up on me, Mama.

Love,
Addison

February 4th

Dear Mama,

The nurses say I've regressed a lot more since I came in. They're saying I'm having trouble keeping my grip on reality.

Last night I looked outside at the crescent moon and it hit me in the head, it hurt so bad, Mama, you wouldn't believe it. And I refused to do anything all day after that. I don't think any of these nurses know what that feels like, I was really upset about it. They're saying I'm getting worse, but everything is real to me, they don't understand. The lying nurses are also mad that I started refusing to take my meds because I know they're poison. Poisoning my body! Lying nurses!

During art therapy, I refused to paint my stress because it was so overwhelming and the paintbrushes were all looking at me in a wicked way. The nurse came over and put her hand on my shoulder. The voices told me to not let her do that, she knows about me. She knows if you're lying. She knows you're worthless.

I stripped her arm off my shoulder really hard and she let out a welp like a dog whose tail was stepped on, and then the white suits came in and I thrashed around as they grabbed me and picked me up. I don't like being touched like this!

Then they brought me into an exam room and laid me down on a cold table. The white suits held me down and I kept screaming. I could feel the hot tears streaming down my cheeks. My throat hurt so bad, it was so sore like I had swallowed a sludge of spicy chili.

There was a bright light and then a pair of glasses and then a piece of wood went into my mouth and things that felt like suction cups were put on my head and then everything inside of me started burning.

I felt a complete nothingness, and my brain was calmed down and I was no longer the terrifying Addison terrorizing everyone during art therapy.

Oh, man. This all sounds so bad, Mama, but I promise I'm not a monster! I'm a nice, polite girl, I promise you that. It's these stupid voices and these stupid nurses and the wicked faces I see everywhere.

I promise I'm a nice, well-behaved girl. And when you come pick me up from this place and tell them that I'm not a monster, then we can go get those big juicy burgers at Scooter's that spit their guts out when you sink your teeth into them. And I promise to always say please and thank you, and be grateful when you do things for me and apologize when I know I've done something wrong, oh please, Mama!

I hope you read this letter.

Love,
Addison

February 10th

Dear Mama,

My brain has calmed down a bit. The voices aren't talking so much. I couldn't write for a while because I couldn't think of the words. They're slowly coming back to me now.

I also thought it would be good for me to write more because I don't know how much longer I'll be able to write. Last night while I was asleep, I felt a tap on my shoulder which startled me. I was scared that it was going to be the suits surrounding my bed, ready to tie me back to the radiator. And if it was, I was ready to holler and scream and wake everybody up. I wanted everyone to see what they were gonna do to me. But thankfully it wasn't the suits. It was Joe the janitor, and he gave me such a kind smile.

You left this in the bathroom, he said, then handed me my sheet of paper and pencil. I was writing a letter to you in the bathroom,

Mama. It's safe there, but I must've forgotten to grab it. Things were getting blurry and the sink was oozing away.

I think it's important for you to have this, Joe said to me. Then he gave me a sweet smile and went back to emptying the garbage cans. I'm so thankful for Joe. If the suits found this letter, I don't know what would've happened.

They started serving cornbread at dinner and it was quite good. I finally found a food that won't make me throw up. I wish Margot stayed long enough to eat it with me. They transferred her to another ward yesterday. I asked the nurses for her address because I wanted to write to her after I got out but they refused to give it to me, saying I shouldn't be writing letters anyway.

I need to get out of here. They want me to live here like a sedated dog, just like Margot. They don't want me to move around so much. They want me to stay put. They'll tell you a rolling stone gathers no moss, but they won't tell you that the moss sucks on the stone until it deteriorates. Edward told me that during Leisure Time. He also told me about the Records Department in the basement, and that I could possibly find your old file down there. I can find your name and your address and then I can escape out of here and find you.

Margot's gone and Dad still doesn't answer the phone. I doubt he even remembers my name. I have nothing left. I hate myself so much. I know deep down inside I'm good, but there's something in there that hurts. I remember one day I was swinging on a tire outside. I was wearing my favorite pair of jean overalls with a daisy-patterned undershirt and the sun was a beautiful ring of warmth and the meadow smelled of fresh dew. I was swinging really high until the voices started yelling at me and my hands slipped. I fell hard on the ground and got a big cut on my arm. I saw the red ooze coming out of it. And then I started picking at my cut, taking off the skin. I hate this skin! I kept yelling, and I kept peeling it off like it was a smooth piece of tape, trying to find whatever was underneath it. But I just saw more blood and veins and muscles and nothing else. I didn't see the good I had inside. I just saw more of me. Hideous and disgusting. I tried to dig deeper, but then some lady grabbed me and we went to the hospital. The good is in there, I just don't know where.

Oh, Mama. I feel so abandoned.

Dad used to say that you abandoned us, that when you saw in my eyes that I was sick, you left us, but I don't believe it. It's not true. I don't believe it!

You would never do that.

You're not Dad.

You wouldn't drop me off at such a horrific place like this for me to rot like an expired apple. To let my pink fleshy insides turn into a putrid brown until I decay into a worthless carcass of my former self. I don't believe it, honest. No matter how many times those words crept out of Dad's revolting lips, I never believed them. You have to trust me on that, Mama. I never believed him. I never will.

Love,
Addison

February 17th

Dear Mama,

I think I've figured it out. It took a long time but I think I have the plan laid out. I've been studying the nurses and the white suits for a while now, checking when they monitor certain places and recognizing which keys they use to open which doors.

I've been on my best behavior recently-taking my medicine, not lashing out, trying my best to participate and comply with the nurses and the white suits. I don't want them to think I'm a threat.

I don't want to feel the nothingness.

I don't want the ice pick.

But I'm behaving very well, Mama. Just know that I'm really good deep down inside. But I have to do some bad things tomorrow so that I can get your file and escape here to come find you. I hope you understand that I have to do this. I hope you don't think I'm a wicked little girl because I'm not. I'm full of love for you. I hope you love me back as much as I do.

For my therapeutic chore tomorrow, I asked the head nurse if I could clean the laundry facilities, which are right down the hall from the Records Department. I told her that the thumping and the smell of detergent was very calming for me, and that the voices went away. The voices, in fact, haven't gone away, and I have been using all my strength to not listen to them. It's so hard Mama, I hope you never have to understand.

The head nurse accepted and said that I would be supervised by one of the white suits.

Then she rang a bell for the sick kids to line up for dinner.

Even with a tray of gruel sitting in front of me, I couldn't resist smiling. I'm just over the moon to get out of here and be with you, Mama! I don't think I'll be able to get my painting of you in time, but just know I painted you so beautifully. Just thinking about you makes a little tear come out of my eye.

The last thing I needed was something heavy. Edward helped me get a heavy round doorknob from God knows who. He told me they replaced them with slanted ones so none of the kids try to hang themselves and they kept the old round knobs in a box in the storage room. He's been eating up my serving of cornbread for the past week in return, knowing that after tomorrow, I wouldn't be back.

I was sitting with him during Leisure Time today. He wasn't playing cards with the other kids. He was playing with his sheets of paper. A bunch of them were crumpled and they littered the table. Before he passed the heavy doorknob to me under the table, he swallowed really hard and his face twitched a little bit. I'll really miss you, he said to me. He said that he had been surrounded by people who praised and cheered him for the most mundane things, but none he could call a friend. He called me his friend, and that wimpy pirate actually made me smile. It was the sweetest thing I ever heard come out of his mouth. Then he took a sheet of paper and folded it into a beautiful crane. It took me a few times to remember how to do it, he said to me. Then he handed it to me under the table with the doorknob.

During the rest of Leisure Time, I was able to finish my book, and it made me want to escape more than ever. The main character was trying to get his little sister to escape this awful world they lived in, but she didn't want to go with him. She was too comfortable. Her whole life was in this world, no matter how awful it was. And everyone around her was comfortable. So the big brother gave up, and he got

comfortable. Until his little sister came and
saved him, so that he could do the same for her.

When I look around the room, I see how
comfortable it can be to stay here. But here, it
is dangerous. Here, they take away your mind
and leave you with your hollow body. It can be
nice to not have the bad things swirl around in
your head anymore, but it is not a true way to
live, Mama. I don't think it is one bit.

Reality always has a way of creeping
itself back inside of you, no matter how many
times you pull it out. If a fire starts in my
room, slowly burning everything to ashes, even if
I take my eyes out of my sockets, I'd still
smell the smoke.

I really liked the story because I think
the author was trying to escape some prison of
his own. And the story made me feel less sad,
because there's someone out there that is
feeling the same way.

I asked the head nurse if we had any
more books by the author but she said she'd
never heard the name, and that she was

surprised that people were even reading the books off the shelves in the Recreation Room. She even admitted that they used some of those books as doorstops.

I was disappointed when she said that, Mama. I liked the story a lot. You should read it too. It helped me see myself not as sick or tormented or diseased, but as a person. A complicated person who needs care and love. And this place has given me neither. It has given me neglect and abuse.

I really hope to meet this Marcus Shelby one day. I think we would have a lot in common. I think he would be very pleasant to talk to.

Now I'm sitting in my bed, writing this letter to you, Mama. And before I can slip it under my mattress to hide, Joe comes by with his garbage cart. He knows I'm not staying here for much longer. You be careful now, he whispers to me. Then he gives me a sweet smile and finishes emptying the last garbage near my bed. He then leaves for the night.

I see Jambo by the windowsill licking his claws clean and waiting for me to give him this letter. I'm gonna slip a piece of paper and my pen in my sock so I can try and write you in case I need to. In case anything were to happen. But that's for tomorrow. Tonight, I feel like I can sleep soundly knowing I will never be here again.

Never. Ever. Again.

Love,
Addison

February 17th

Dear Mama,

I need to make this letter short so I can give it to Jambo. Everything went as planned. I went down to the laundry facility with the white suit and when he was whistling to himself, not looking at me, I slipped that heavy doorknob out of my baggy pants, knocked him over in the head with it, and grabbed his key ring.

One of the keys opened the room to the Records Department, but there's no key that opens the back door in the basement to get out. So I'm trapped here with this white suit on the ground, bleeding from the head, and it's only a matter of time until the other white suits realize I've been gone a while and they start looking for me.

Jambo's waiting by the tiny window in the laundry facility, telling me to hurry up. I need to go and find you.

I will find you, Mama.

I will not give up.

When I get out of here, I can't wait to

Mama,

They're looking for me.

They shut down the whole hospital.

Apparently, they sent a search party outside. They know I have a ring of keys but it's only a matter of time before they realize I never left. I can hear the white suits bicker with each other while I hide in this awful ventilation system. I don't know how long I can hide in here, Mama. And I only have room on this piece of paper for one more letter. Maybe you can come here real quick and talk some sense into them, tell them I'm misunderstood. Please Mama, please help me. I need you.

I hear the shuffling of squeaky boots. I know they're here, they're close, and I know they know I'm here. It's only a matter of time 'till they find me and give me the ice pick, oh Mama, I'm so scared! I'm curling my cold hands around my head, my sweet tormented head. I'm trying to have as many thoughts as I can before they're taken from me. I'm holding onto them as tight as I can like they're a group of balloons and once I let go, they'll float away and I'll never get them back. I know I'll lose my thoughts of you. I know the ice pick will take that away from me and that makes me so scared, you have no idea. Oh, please I hope they'll be easy on me. Maybe they won't give me the ice pick. Maybe they won't find me. I hope they don't find me. I hope I find you first.

I found you.

I found you, Mama.

I found your file.

Mama, I can't believe I found you.

In the middle of the night, I made a dash for the Records Department and went through the files as quick as I could. I found my last name and then I found yours, and what a beautiful name you have, Mama. Much more beautiful than Addison.

But my heart sank when I started reading your file. I read about the car accident, about the damage in those delicate nerves you have in your brain, and those experiments they put you through to try and repair them, only to hurt the delicate nerves in your eyes.

Nothing in this file says they could fix you.

All those letters I had Jambo send to you.

All worthless.

Mama, my heart aches.

I still love you so much. I hope after they find me, they'll find this letter too, and someone with a heart big enough to cool the hottest volcanoes and melt the coldest ice sheets will read it to you. And maybe you can imagine what I looked like. You can use that big, beautiful imagination machine you have in your head.

But I don't want you to do that.

I don't want you to imagine.

I want you to know what I look like.

Even if you'll never be able to see me.

I have long auburn hair that hangs over my shoulders. I usually keep it curly but right now it's frizzy and all knotted up. I have ears that stick out to the sides and earlobes that jiggle when I run. I have very thin, pale lips, and teeth that look like old gravestones because Dad didn't like taking me to the dentist. I have tender, warm-colored skin that bruises easily and needs to be caressed with care. I have thin eyebrows and under them rest a pair of big brown eyes that wish they could see you. And most importantly, Mama, I have a little mole that sits right above my right lip. Just like you.

But I have to stop writing now.

I'm all out of space.

I hear a pair of footsteps coming.

I have to hide this letter so it can be found later.

The door handle is jiggling and in a matter of seconds, it will be open and then everything will stop.

I'm starting to sweat and I can feel the pick before it's even in me. It's already in me, Mama, and once it's in you, it never leaves.

The Freed

"Do you consume? Do you feel joyous when you consume? Or rather, do you feel sick to your bowels? As if you had just eaten a heavy meal. Is every day the same? Is it always the same? When was the last time you were sorrowful or mournful? Do you know what those emotions are?

"We have everything within reach. Technology has led to decadence, to the softening of skin and the swelling of bellies. We are all fragile eggs protected by a delicate shell that's easily breakable, revealing our soft, yolky insides.

"Suffering has no place in Macrosanti.

"We make things that help people get places faster or find food easier or we make things more accessible, easier, softer, faster, more delicate, more gentle, or just outright cheaper. But why would we make anything more horrific? Why would we make anything that makes people depressed or mournful or—"

I looked up from the book. The two marble eyes of the creature stared at me. Its coat smelled of expired eggs. I turned the page and kept reading.

"Why would anyone want to suffer?" I proposed to the creature. It didn't respond.

"Well, we wouldn't," I told the creature.

Its expression was unchanged. It just stood still and kept its confused gaze on me. I kept reading.

"Apathy is the opioid of Macrosanti. Our comfortable consumption has filled us with all of these emotions without us even knowing. And I know you must feel this way because you are still reading these words.

"It is the veiled suppression of these emotions by Macrosanti that keeps its residents hollow inside—but there is hope. A triumphant hope you must hold on to for as long as you live. The hollowness is not something to feel misery about, for when one revives their own heart, to let it beat freely with passion and love, those beats are echoed throughout the entire body."

I said the last word with a touch of bravado, but the creature just stood there, flailing its tail behind it. Its marble eyes looked at me, confused or intrigued, I wasn't sure. Then it let out a wailing *moooo!* and trudged away, disappearing into the nearby forest. I decided to finish reading.

"Understand this: the natural world is out there and right now, you're breathing the air of the unnatural.

"They told us that the rest of the world was uninhabitable, that Macrosanti was our safe haven. That the terrain was too harsh for our supple skin and that the mountains were too hard for our fragile bones. They even built the lookout point for us to see so that we may never have the urge to leave.

"But I don't believe it.

"I never believed it.

"My father used to tell me stories about the forests and the mountains and the lakes, which were stories his father told him, which he heard from his father, and so on.

"On page 94, I drew a map of the rest of the world. I've never left Macrosanti, neither has my father or any of his ancestors, but I know in my heart that this is not everything.

"There's more. There must be more. My heart yearns for it. And I know yours does too."

I closed the book and I rested against the trunk of the tree, knobs of protruding wood poked into my back. Almost a natural massage.

Today, I knew I would die.

There was no fight in me.

Or even life for that matter.

Nature had aged me quickly, or I must have caught one of her nasty diseases. My heartbeat was slow like the ticking hand of a grandfather clock. My bones were brittle and fragile as if they could snap at any moment. Deep pouches rested under my eyes and my hair that used to be black, then white, was now gray and dirty.

My mind was sharp. I could speak well, even eloquently at times in my low and raspy voice, but speaking didn't keep you alive, and I knew that all too well. The heart doesn't beat to the vibrations in your throat. And it's so unfortunate how someone could die even though they were perfectly capable of speaking, and they would have had so much more to say if time allowed it. Speaking was the only thing I could do, but it was the last thing I wanted to do.

It's quite unfortunate for someone to die on such an ugly day. A gray blanket of clouds swallowed the radiant blue sky as only patches of it poked out. A winter fog rolled through the canyon and clumps of snow started to materialize on the rocks. No man should take his last breath on a day where the sky showed no sun. But I could not control this, either.

A vehicle, one I've seen before used by the patrollers, was coming toward me, kicking up pebbles from the dirt.

They've already come a few times to try and convince us to come back. You must understand that anyone is allowed to leave Macrosanti. There are no handcuffs or imprisonments for leaving. But as you can imagine, residents of Macrosanti lie in an excess of stimulation and comfort, making it difficult to leave—especially when a wasteland surrounds the dome for farther than the naked eye can see.

We were miles away from Macrosanti now. Far enough that we couldn't see the dome anymore. Many years ago when we climbed down the ragged stairs from the lookout point and made our way through the wasteland, we kept turning back in awe at the size of the dome, which glimmered so horrifically in the sunlight. An enormous monstrosity.

No matter how far we traveled, however, the patrollers would still find us by tracking us through the chip in our arm. It was put there when we were born. It was for our protection in case we went missing. It stays in there for the rest of your life, but they'll tell you it's only used in emergency situations. Ellie wasn't too fond of being tracked anymore so we cut hers out of her.

The patrollers came and they beckoned us to come back. They told us about all the new and amazing things happening in Macrosanti. They've come to us plenty of times already. One time they came to tell us about the

Companion X. "Twice as fast, and virtually no buffer between snippets!" one of the patrollers said with beguiled enthusiasm. We told them we weren't interested. Another time, they came to tell us about all the new products at the mega-markets. Blackwheat butter bread, molten jello sticks, and eighteen new types of flavoring paste. We told them we weren't interested. No matter how many times we told them, they kept coming until we decided that this would be the last time they would come.

I felt a sharp pang in my chest as the doors of the vehicle hinged up and opened, and three pairs of black boots stepped out. The patrollers cautiously walked toward me. They all wore the black boots, it didn't matter whose feet they were on. They were all the same.

The footsteps stopped, the boots halted right next to me I could almost smell the rubber, and I looked up into his eyes.

"My God, what happened to you?" one of them asked.

I didn't respond.

I was covered in blood.

Ellie's blood.

"Are you okay?" one of them asked.

I didn't respond. They just stood there, hands on hips, looking at each other in confusion. You must understand that it was quite difficult for me to speak since I was so ill.

"Where's your sister, Mordecai?"

"Dead," I croaked.

They looked unconvinced, so I took off my blood-stained shirt and handed it to one of them.

"If you don't believe me, run the blood tests. It'll match. It's hers."

"What happened?"

"She was delirious from the heat and took a tumble off that cliff over there."

I pointed to the steep rock edge, miles away from us. Below the cliff was a hungry body of water, which would have swallowed Ellie's body, giving them no way to find it.

"How did you get her blood on your—"

"I was trying to revive her."

"You went all the way down that cliff to—"

"Yes, and I'd throw myself over that cliff if it would save her."

The patrollers scratched their chins.

Their lips started moving, and I didn't listen to a word that came out. When I saw that he wasn't looking at me, I darted my eyes over to a shrub that I knew Ellie was hiding behind. I slowly raked my fingers through my scalp, signaling for her to escape through the forest. I imagined her running through the trees ever so quietly so she wouldn't be heard, holding the leaves over her bleeding arm. And I would've cut my tracker out too, but that wouldn't stop them from trying to find us. They had to know she was gone, and they had to hear those words come from me.

The lips on the patroller stopped moving. Then a pair of hands lifted me from under my shoulders to bring me into the vehicle and back to the world of software over soil. Of gadgets over gardens. Of lithium over light.

My heart was content.

It didn't matter that they were going to bring me back, because by the time I was back in the dome, I'd have already expired, and Ellie would be too deep in the forest for them to ever find her.

Sam Calvo

A Note From The Author

Thank you for reading my novel. It took a great deal of time to write and I sincerely appreciate you taking the time to read it. If you liked (or didn't like) the novel, please consider leaving an honest review on Amazon or Goodreads or by going to samcalvo.com/review

Until we meet again for the next story...

Sincerely,

Sam Calvo

The Tree In The Town Square

THE TREE
IN THE
TOWN SQUARE

a short story collection by
SAM CALVO

Available at samcalvo.com/novels

About the Author

Sam Calvo is the author of the philosophical and magical realist novel, *My Isabel: A Story of Reflection and Understanding* and the unconventional collection of short stories, *The Tree In The Town Square*. Sam currently resides in Seattle, Washington.

If you would like to get in touch with Sam Calvo, please send an email to *sam@samcalvo.com* or go to *samcalvo.com*

Acknowledgments

Thank you to all my supporters

Tricia Harris   Gabby Sitrin   Shauna Goldman

Sonia Rashid   George Pierce Caitlin Connors

Kate Gevanthor   Paulina Grekov   Dillon Bromley

Haley Phillips   Allie Scott   Yael Egnal

Noa Kretchmer   Ariel Kesterke   Frank Fink

Brenna Fowler   Vicky Pluck   Kevin Petnuch

Hannah Portoff   Hannah Barton   Caroline Motzer

Anna Perez   Yuwon   Miguel Reyes

Joseph Goddall   Meg McIntyre   Hannah Emcez

Made in the USA
Las Vegas, NV
09 May 2022